THE SEVENTH GUEST

THE SEVENTH GUEST

Gaston Boca

Translated by John Pugmire

The Seventh Guest

First published in French in 1935 by
Librairie Gallimard as *Les Invités de minuit*
Copyright © Librairie Gallimard, 1935.
THE SEVENTH GUEST
English translation copyright © by John Pugmire 2018.

Every effort has been made to trace the holders of copyright. In the event of any inadvertent transgression of copyright, the editor would like to hear from the author's representatives. Please contact me at pugmire1@ yahoo.com.

FIRST AMERICAN EDITION
Library of Congress Cataloguing-in-Publication Data
Boca, Gaston
[*Les Invités de minuit* English]
The Seventh Guest / Gaston Boca
Translated from the French by John Pugmire

To Roland and Danièle, with infinite thanks.

9

INTRODUCTION: THE FRENCH GOLDEN AGE

To my knowledge, there is no accepted definition of a French locked room Golden Age, but—despite the isolated activities of Gaston Leroux in 1907-08; Boileau-Narcejac as a team in the 1950s; Martin Méroy in the 1960s; and the one-man Golden Age of Paul Halter starting in the 1980s—it is hard to deny that the preponderance of authors and titles occurred between 1930 and 1948. Much of the information below comes from the excellent bibliography *1000 Chambres Closes,* by Roland Lacourbe *et al.*

1930 saw the appearance of Pierre Véry's *Le Testament de Basil Crookes* (The Testament of Basil Crookes), and 1948 was the year that Thomas Narcejac's *La Mort est du voyage* (Death on Board) won the *Grand Prix du Roman d'aventures*, France's international award for mystery fiction (He and Boileau met at Narcejac's award dinner.)

The period between those years saw three prolific authors: Maurice Leblanc, Noël Vindry and the Belgian Stanislas-André Steeman; Pierre Boileau and Thomas Narcejac writing separately; and many of what Roland Lacourbe calls "meteors of the night"—authors who produced one or two books in a very short period, then disappeared from sight.

Maurice Leblanc is best known for his short stories featuring ArsèneLupin, but his gentleman thief also appears in two novels: La Barre-y-va (The Barre-y-va) in 1932, and *La Femme aux deux sourires* (The Woman With Two Smiles) in 1933.

Of Steeman'smore than thirty novels, five contained locked room puzzles: *Six homes morts* (Six Dead Men) and *La Nuit du 12 au 13* (The Night of the 12th and 13th) in 1931; *Zéro* (Zero) in 1932; *L'Ennemi sans visage* (The Enemy Without a Face) in 1934; and *L'Infaillible Silas Lord* (The Infallible Silas Lord) in 1938.

Vindry also wrote more than thirty novels, but is best known for his ten locked room mysteries, of which three—*La Maison qui tue* (The House That Kills) in 1932; *La Bête hurlante* (The Howling Beast) and *Le Double Alibi* (The Double Alibi), both in 1934—have already been published by LRI. Two other of his works: *La Fuite des morts*

*(*The Vanishing Dead) in 1933 and *À travers les murailles* (Through the Walls) in 1937 are also very highly rated.

Pierre Boileau wrote *La Pierre qui tremble* (The Trembling Stone) in 1934; *Le Repos de Bacchus* (Bacchus in Repose), which won the *Grand Prix du Roman d'aventures,* in 1938; his masterpiece *Six Crimes Sans Assassin* (literally Six Crimes Without a Killer) in 1935; writing as Anicot, *Un Assassin au chateau* (A Killer in the Castle) in 1944; and *L'Assassin vient les mains vides* (The Killer Comes Empty-Handed) in 1945. In addition to the aforementioned *La Mort est du voyage,* Narcejac also wrote *L'Assassin de Minuit (*The Midnight Killer*)* in 1945.

Amongst the meteors of the night, in alphabetical order, are:

-Gaston Boca, who wrote four novels between 1933 and 1935, of which two, *L'Ombre sur le jardin* (The Shadow Over the Garden) in1933, and *Les Invités de minuit* (The Seventh Guest) in 1935, are regarded as early classics. The remaining two: *Les Usines de l'effroi* (The Terror Factories) in1934,and *Le Dîner de Mantes* (Dinner at Mantes) in 1935, both have weak solutions.

-Antoine Chollier who wrote *Dossier n°7* (Dossier n°7) in 1946.

-Alexis Gensoul, who wrote *L'Énigma de Tefaha* (The Riddle of Tefaha)*; Gribouille est mort* (Gribouille Is Dead); and—with Charles Garnier—*La Mort vient de nulle part* (Death out of Nowhere), all in 1945, whilst a conscript in the French army.

-Michel Herbert and EugèneWyl, who together wrote *La Maison interdite* (The Forbidden House) in 1932; and *Le Crime derrière la porte* (The Crime Behind the Door) in 1934.

-Maurice Lanteaume, who wrote *Orage sur la Grande Semaine* (Storm Over Festival Week) in 1944, whilst in a German concentration camp; *Trompe-l'œil* (Trompe-l'Œil) in 1946; and *La Treizième balle* (The Thirteenth Bullet) in 1948.

-Roch de Santa-Maria who wrote *Pendu trop court* (Hanged Too Short) in 1937, based on a real-life impossible crime.

Several of the foregoing novels may well be candidates for future LRI publication.

Gaston Bocahut, who wrote as Gaston Boca, wrote four novels and one short story in quick succession at the beginning of the French Golden Age of detective fiction, and was never heard from again,

8

which caused some to speculate that the books had been written by a more celebrated author under a pseudonym.

But Bocahut's "secret" was that he was a highly-qualified engineer who had graduated from one of France's top schools, the École Centrale, and wished to pursue a career in industry. He had dabbled in writing during the obligatory (at the time) military service, during weekends when there was little else to do. But, once he was back in civil life, as assistant director of a factory in the dreary Paris suburb of Nanterre, he was too busy during the week to write. And, on weekends, he preferred to take the number 158 tramway to more charming spots such as St. Germain and Bougival, in pursuit of the delectable company of the opposite sex. Writing detective fiction was the lowest of his priorities.

Nevertheless, Roland Lacourbe, the noted French locked room expert and publisher of numerous anthologies, says of Boca's works:

"By their subtlety, their invention, their popular inspiration—which unfailingly makes us think of another celebrated Gaston—and their sense of foreboding... the four novels offer brilliant variations on our favourite theme. Not forgetting that the date of their appearance... makes Gaston Boca one of the great French pioneers of the genre."

Boca's dilettante detective, Stéphane Triel, who calls himself "a collector of tragic trifles," seems closer to Leroux's Joseph Rouletabille than to Sherlock Holmes, but his confidant, the journalist Luc Dutheil, is every bit as clueless as Dr. Watson.

Regarding *The Seventh Guest* itself, seldom have I read a more monstrous and intricate plot.

A note about Boca's very personal style: a distinct preference for strings of sentences rather than paragraphs, creating a stream-of-consciousness effect; and suddenly jumping from past tense to present, to give a scene a sense of urgency.

John Pugmire   New York, 2018

10

FIRST PART

CHAPTER I

The invitation

Apart from a certain tendency, as a family, for the protagonists to kill each other, this is not your classic tragedy. So why did chance, that strange stage manager, respect the three unities of action, space and time?

That park surrounded by insurmountable walls, and that cold spring night were certainly full of action. How much fear and dread was packed into those acres in those few hours!

For that reason, I wanted to call this account of mine "Just One Night." But Danièle said it sounded like a love story.

I ask you!

As if only a woman could leave her mark on a night.

Anyway, I shan't forget that night for a very long time, even though there were no amorous adventures. What am I saying? I never even went to bed at all.

At all the most thrilling moments, I was sitting in an armchair.

There was a woman, I must confess, and a pretty one—even though rather pale. But she was in another armchair.

And we stayed where we were, even after the lights went out.

A long spring night, for sure, if you generously count it from dusk to dawn.

But, still, just one night.

*****

It's the letter that was the cause of it all.

Actually, no. It's the sunshine that started it.

The first real sunshine of the year, at the end of March, made its appearance at five o'clock in the evening, between heavy storm clouds. The yellow light of summer against a wintery background. Something unexpected, seductive, and fragile.

I opened the window. One corner of the sky, beyond the zinc roofs, was as blue as a box of sugar-coated pills. Above me, the buds of the chestnut trees shone with a sticky brilliance.

I heard Triel's voice behind my back:

'Close the window,' it said, with its inflections that were so familiar and so dear to me. 'We're freezing here, with your radiator which doesn't work.'

I replied something about the charm of the Parisian spring, made up like a girl of easy virtue.

That was the moment the concierge chose to bring the letter.

If ever a letter deserved the black edging of mourning, it was that one.

But it was made up as well.

The envelope, exuding the scent of an unidentified perfume, was the colour of lilacs in bloom. The handwriting was delicate, feminine and charming.

To the point that I read the address twice, to make sure there was no error.

Messieurs Luc Dutheil et Stéphane Triel
11, Boulevard Raspail
PARIS

'I hate it when they address envelopes as if we're a couple. Anyone would think I was part of the furniture. That's what you get when you frequent men of letters.'

Such was Triel's reaction to the perfumed missive. It's true he wasn't in a particularly good mood that afternoon. He was tackling the umpteenth volume of *Rocambole* and things were starting to get complicated.

'That's not the question,' I said, bouncing the envelope on the back of my hand.

Good news or bad news?

I knew very well that kind of question was guaranteed to exasperate my friend Triel, who professes that every event, by the complex nature of its consequences, is good *and* bad, not good *or* bad.

'Good news or bad news, eh?'

'Close the window and open the envelope.'

And that's what I did. After which, I read the letter in silence, ten feet away from him.

My eyes must have widened in surprise, for Triel abandoned Ponson du Terrail for an instant.

'What is it?'

'What?' I replied, happy to take my revenge. 'Are you questioning me? Aren't you Triel the clairvoyant any more? Doesn't your radioactive gaze penetrate envelopes any longer?'

'How am I supposed to know why that woman from Marly called for our help?'

'Ah, so you deduced that much.'

'Yes.'

I stayed silent for a moment.

'That's marvellous.'

Triel turned completely towards me. His angular features were in silhouette against the evening sun.

'No,' he said, 'it's child's play. The letter is addressed to us collectively, so that there's little chance it's a love letter, is there?'

'Obviously.'

'Furthermore, we don't know the woman: her handwriting and her perfume mean nothing to us. She, on the other hand, knows our names, which have only been associated with one another in crime reports.

'The fact that the handwriting is trembling and hasty, and the blotting has been done so hurriedly that the ink has spread, confirm my theory.

'This woman obtained your address from the office of your newspaper. She wrote to both of us at the same address, thinking that we formed an inseparable couple: Castor Dutheil and Pollux Triel.'

'My dear old Pollux,' I replied, overcome with glee, 'you should write detective stories. It's quite clear that the little story you improvised has nothing whatever to do with reality. Nothing!'

'But it's romantic. And seductive.

'Continue, Triel. What are we going to do for the little lady of Marly?'

Irritated, he tore the letter from my hands.

He read:

Dear Friends,
My husband and I are travelling through France. We would be very grateful if you could spare us a few days. If you can, please come to Nanteuil right away. I will be very happy to receive you, and my husband is anxious to make your acquaintance.

Cordially yours,

JEANNE

The address was:

Jeanne d'Arlon, Nanteuil Manor, near Marly, Seine-et-Oise.

'Aha!' said Triel, looking up. 'Now we're friends with ladies of the manor, are we?'

'Me? No, I....'

Up until then, I'd been happy enough pulling Triel's leg. Now, my attention was on the text of the letter itself.

'Are you sure it wasn't you who...,' I asked.

Triel shrugged his shoulders and I dropped the subject.

Jeanne d'Arlon, Nanteuil Manor, near Marly, Seine-et-Oise.

I made a great intellectual effort.

'I did know a Jeanne once,' I said, racking my brains. 'She was a conductress on the Louvre-Versailles line.'

It was an old French tramline.

From there to lady of the manor was quite a stretch....

'Have you got a telephone directory?' asked Triel.

'No.'

'Then we'd better go to the *bistro*.'

He put on his Basque beret and we left.

Neither *Au Rendezvous des Chauffeurs* nor *À la Toison d'Or* had a phone directory. It was only at the post office in the rue de la Glacière that we were able to consult the Bottin *Who's Who*, with its grey binding. Triel made a note in his pocket-book:

D'Arlon (Comte René) et Comtesse, née *Jeanne de Nanteuil,*

16

followed by a symbol of a little house with two gables, indicating they were the owners of Nanteuil Manor. Make a note of it, Triel.

And then, another address. That's amazing…

Make a note of it, anyway: *15 Avenue Catinat, Saigon, Indo-Chine.*

'Well,' said Triel, closing his pocket-book, 'all that seems clear enough. A young lady from Nanteuil married one M. d'Arlon, who does business in the Far East. And, from time to time, they both come to spend their holidays in the lady's family home.'

What has that got to do with us….

'Isn't there a telephone at this manor?'

'No.'

We left the post office.

'There is one solution,' I said. 'We could just go there. What are you doing tonight?'

'Oh!' said Triel, shocked. 'So soon, that just wouldn't be right.'

The sky above rue de la Glacière turned blue . The sun was reflected in the window of a grocery shop, a reminder of the beautiful days of summer, when the asphalt glistened after the last shower.

'Decidedly, spring is in the air, this evening,' I said.

'We haven't got a car any more,' said Triel. 'What's left of it is on the road to Montereau.'

'We'll take the tram.'

'Just think, Triel, soon the sky will turn pink. A spring evening is on the way. Tomorrow morning, we'll be awakened by the sound of birds chirping in the grounds of the manor.

'And, from the metro at la Glacière, it's only one change for Maillot.'

Triel allowed himself to be persuaded.

I maintain what I said before: it was the sun that was the cause of it. Without it, without all the off-season fantasies, we wouldn't have gone to Nanteuil until the next day, or the day after, or never….

In any case, we wouldn't have spent *that particular night* in Nanteuil.

CHAPTER II

The footprints

It was an orchard, a wrought iron garden, that manor gate. It was nothing but spirals, undulating bars and metal flowers.

'Indisputably, one of the most beautiful gates of the XVIIIth century,' I'd observed to Triel, for his education.

But one can get tired of anything, and, after waiting for ten minutes in front of it, the metal motifs were starting to burn into our eyeballs.

Behind us lay the dirt road which ran along a ridge between market gardens, on which the rays of the sun, already low in the sky, were trained like a projector.

On the other side of the gate was a wooded park, awash in a shadow which the first leaves were starting to colour green. Budding lilacs, honeysuckle, and silence....

'It's Sleeping Beauty's castle,' I said, pulling the handle of the door bell for the third time.

The steel wire attached to the wall shivered and a derisory cracked tinkling could be heard two metres away.

No one appeared.

It was very bizarre. The concierge's lodge, clearly visible through the gate, was close by, and there was smoke coming out of the chimney.

'Some concierge,' I said, 'cooking food and leaving visitors waiting.'

'Yoohoo!' called Triel.

I cocked an ear.

'Someone replied,' I said.

'Do you think so?'

'Seemed like it.'

'Maybe an echo.'

Triel called out again.

There was no response—and no echo.

'Wait,' I said. 'I can see another way in, perhaps more practicable than that insolent gate.'

There was indeed a small door in the boundary wall, very close to us. It opened at a touch.

'Are you coming, Stéphane?'

'Bah,' said Triel. 'After all, we were invited.'

The impression of magnificence created by the great gate dissipated rapidly on the other side. What appeared to be the main drive, which disappeared round a curve almost immediately, had been passably raked. But a thick layer of dead leaves covered the minor paths, which disappeared into the trees. Scattered around the concierge's lodge itself, a fragile and elegant building modelled after the Petit Trianon, were bits of plaster from the walls and loose slates from the roof.

I tapped on one of the mildewed window panes. No response.

The door was ajar. We went in.

In the first room—the dining room—a piece of knitting on the table, a pair of spectacles, a folded newspaper. To the left, two interconnecting rooms. Everything was in order, including the properly made beds. A Christ on the cross was stretched out on mauve-flowered wallpaper.

To the right, in the kitchen, a pot was bubbling on the stove. I lifted the lid, but there were only potatoes dancing ponderously in the clouds of steam. The water was threatening to dry up, so I added another saucepanful.

'The presence of potatoes,' I observed, 'indicates that the inhabitants lack a refined taste.'

'Shh,' said Triel. 'Listen....'

I replaced the lid carefully on the pot.

'Did you hear it?'

'Maybe... vaguely... A cry, was it?'

'Something like that.'

We waited on the doorstep.

There was a slight breeze, bringing with it, mingled with the sound of whispering leaves, a sort of long cry with indiscernible syllables.

'A name, no doubt.'

'That explains it,' I said. 'The concierge has lost his cat.'

Triel tapped mechanically on the windowpane.

'So,' he said, 'let's find the cat—and the concierge at the same time!'

I closed the door behind me.

We walked towards the undergrowth.

I put my hand in my jacket pocket and felt paper crinkle under my touch: the lilac letter.

Was it really such good news that letter had brought us?

I looked questioningly at Triel, but he was pushing ahead with long strides, his nose to the wind, on full alert: Triel, or the inspired onlooker.

*****

At best, it could have passed for a pleasant walk.

The cries had stopped. We directed ourselves by guesswork towards that area of the park from which they had come the moment before. It was not the same direction as the manor, as far as we could tell from the main drive.

The sun's rays were now like long, horizontal arrows piercing the foliage. Under our feet, the ground, still wet from a recent shower, made a soft sound like a compressed sponge.

One roundabout, two roundabouts... a small pond full of dead leaves and branches... we were obviously in the most abandoned part of the park. The oaks seemed afflicted by a complicated form of rheumatism. Tribes of nettles invaded the paths....

'Can you hear it?'

The question was superfluous.

They weren't long cries thrown to the winds any more, but short, sharp moans which choked in a few moments for lack of breath. The voice sounded hoarse, like an old woman's. And it was there, close by....

Triel, as if driven by the release of a spring, leapt over a bush and headed in that direction. I followed a short distance behind.

One hundred yards, covered in excellent style. The cries start to fade. Triel accelerates; I accelerate even more, with the result that I collide with him when he suddenly stops dead.

We are at the edge of a clearing. In front of us is a birch tree. And, leaning against its trunk, is the moaning woman. She doesn't even turn her head to look at us, at the strangers rushing towards her.

She's moaning very quietly. Is she going to die there, perhaps?

21

She's bareheaded, with a grey face and black hair tied in a bun. She's wearing a long blue apron splashed with mud. It's obviously the concierge. She's the one who left the potatoes boiling in the pot just now.

'What is it? Are you wounded?'

Her hands are cold. There's no blood to be seen, and no sign of a fight.

She turns her head slightly without seeing us, then continues to stare ahead.

What's she looking at, like that?

A hundred yards away, through the trees, a small wood cabin. A tool shed, apparently. Yes, I can see it... So what?

It's a bit dilapidated, but there's nothing frightful about it.

Except....

Except—and I look down at the ground and discover it at the same time as Triel: footprints going towards the cabin. Large prints of clogs, sunk deep, already half full of water.

The prints go as far as the cabin, *but they don't come back.*

'Triel, those prints—.'

'Yes, I see.'

It's a drama unfolding before our eyes, in a pithy turn of phrase.

We both have the instinctive reaction to run to the cabin, where the man in the clogs might be lying in agony. We pause when we see the woman, no longer supported, slide down the trunk and fall on her knees in the mud.

I lean towards her. I hear the name on her lips:

'Benoît....'

'Benoît,' I say. 'That was it. Those were the two syllables in the cries we heard.'

'Look out!' says Triel.

Two individuals are coming towards us at a rapid clip. Very rapid. Decidedly, the park is filling up. It's as if there's a tragic rally with that cabin as the objective.

The first is in riding boots and breeches, and the second is in a blue uniform. The lord of the manor and his chauffeur, presumably.

The former makes an effort to recover his breath, then shouts, in a harsh voice:

'Who are you? What are you doing here?'

22

He is young, thin, and exasperated, and his black eyes shine like a pen just out of the inkwell. The chauffeur is a scrawny Vietnamese.

'And, first of all, let go of that woman!'

Triel doesn't move, but I blush. What must we look like, bending over this fifty-year-old who only fainted after filling the park with her cries? Like two satyrs, perhaps?

The one in boots is holding a riding crop in his right hand. If he raises that hand, Triel will knock him senseless and the chauffeur will jump on us like a tiger.

A couple of explanations that I offer, while the concierge's head is resting on my knees, avert a confrontation. We introduce ourselves. The newcomer—M. d'Arlon, as I had suspected—extends us his right hand, after having transferred the riding crop to his left.

'My apologies, gentlemen... I couldn't have imagined....'

His words are courteous, but the look he gives us is far from friendly. As for the chauffeur, ten feet away, he's impassive and almost at attention.

'Tell me,' asks d'Arlon, 'were you hunting my concierge?'

'No,' I say, 'we were drawn by her cries.'

'I heard them as well... but she didn't cry out alone, I believe.'

Triel points to the footprints, and d'Arlon stops at once. He's understood. He even knows more than we do, for he stops us with a gesture.

'Yes,' he says, 'I understand.'

He nods his head.

'Distressing, distressing... what unfortunate circumstances in which to meet.'

The words contrast with the indifference of his tone. This d'Arlon is a decidedly out-of- tune individual.

'Émile,' he says to the chauffeur, 'take this poor woman back to her lodge, and, above all, make sure she doesn't leave. She mustn't see what we're about to see. Will you come with me, gentlemen?'

'Certainly.'

While Émile retreats, carrying with him, for better or for worse, the concierge, who is twice as heavy as he is, we step on to the virgin ground surrounding the cabin. Our steps leave imprints on the wet clay: *the first to do so since the clog prints.*

'What a sad story!' continues d'Arlon meanwhile. 'That woman is

23

the concierge of the estate. You've realised as much, I'm sure. She lives in the lodge by the gate, with her husband, Old Fougeras, and her nephew, Benoît Gérapin.

'Now, Benoît disappeared last night. And his relatives learnt this morning that he hadn't been seen in the village... and that he'd even failed to turn up for a rendezvous last night....

'So, since this morning, they've been looking for him in the park.

'And, *voilà*... He's here. Such a lively fellow!'

CHAPTER III

The perfume of the lady in grey

We have reached the cabin.

The door is ajar. Triel pushes it with a kick, takes a step forward, and stops. D'Arlon and I join him by his side.

Darkness. And a long, rigid shape forming a vertical line in the darkness. A sort of puppet with broken joints... Enough with the euphemisms: a hanged man.

'That's him, all right,' says d'Arlon.

The corpse's limbs are already cold. When we touch it, it swings at the end of its rope. It spins round and looks at us, face to face, with a macabre sneer.

'Death occurred about twenty hours ago,' guesses Triel.

Which no one contests.

We try to take down the cadaver, but it's no easy task. The large body weighs heavily on the rough rope. And none of us has a cutting tool.

'Just a moment,' says d'Arlon. 'I'll get a knife.'

He runs out.

Triel and I remain in a *tête-à-tête* with the vertical remains of Benoît Gérapin.

What a reception, for our first visit to Nanteuil!

Everything is tidy in the hanged man's little house.

The jacket, collar and tie are properly folded on a workbench. A rose is starting to fade in the buttonhole, but no petal has yet fallen.

'As if there were no struggle,' I say.

Triel gives me a look which says:

"Why would there be a struggle, you idiot?"

And, effectively, to overcome and hang up the strapping fellow swinging in front of us would have taken at least six assailants. Assailants who would have left no trace in the surrounding mud.

Of course there hadn't been a struggle! It was a suicide, a vulgar suicide.

So, if that's the case, why am I feeling ill at ease, confused and anxious? Is it just the sight of the corpse? I've seen dead people in my time, and far uglier.

Is it because Triel is trying to sniff out trouble and look for footprints on the tiled floor, like a hunting dog?

What is it that's bothering me?

Now I seem to detect an odour in the cabin. Not the odour of death. On the contrary. A scent, and a very delicate one. Vague, admittedly, and one I couldn't describe... But a scent already known to me.

I approach Benoît Gérapin. The scent doesn't come from his clothes. It floats about him... It suggests a vanished presence, a rapid passage through the air of the cabin, leaving behind a perfumed wake.

For there are no flowers blossoming here. And the rose in the buttonhole is almost odourless.

I would share my impression with Triel, if he were in the mood to listen.

But Triel, who continues to forage everywhere, doesn't say a word, and I know he has a horror of others speaking when he himself doesn't deign to.

He's been roaming around outside, all around the cabin. He's been crawling on all fours on the ground. He's even—and I'm not making this up—*taken the temperature of the water in the indentations.* Yes, he placed his finger in one of those minuscule puddles with the careful air of a housewife checking her *bain-marie.*

Now, he's standing face-to-face with the hanged man, seemingly in a competition to see who can stay silent the longest. He's staring hard at a point under his nose, which doesn't seem called for.

He's even gone so far as to take his handkerchief out of his pocket and gently wipe the dead man's lips with it. After which, he studies the handkerchief.

I go over to look at it myself, and discover , on the white linen, a clear trace of red.

'Blood?' I ask.

'No. Lipstick.'

And it's true.

I'm taken aback.

'That's incredible!' I gasp.

He puts his handkerchief back in his pocket.

'Why?' he asks.

Apparently it's the done thing, nowadays.

I take another look at Benoît Gérapin. His smile has changed. Without his make-up, he's purplish and lugubrious.

And it seems to me that another whiff of perfume is coming my way.

That perfume which wasn't brought in by him... That lipstick....

I take a step back. This purple, made-up, scented victim fills me with horror.

The sun has gone down to the level of the bushes. An enormous bloody eye, which seems to be spying on us.

The light penetrates the cabin and creates a trapezium on the floor in the shape of a guillotine.

I know, now, where I've breathed that perfume before: on lilac-coloured notepaper!

'Triel,' I ask. 'Don't you smell a particular odour here?'

'No,' he replies absent-mindedly. 'I caught a head cold in your room.

'What does it smell of?'

'It seems to me...,' I start to say.

But I stop.

A shadow has fallen across the room, inside the illuminated guillotine.

We turn round.

A young woman is there, framed by the doorway and silent, as if brought by the rays of sunlight. She is bare-headed and wrapped in a large coat. The sunlight creates a fawn halo above her brown hair.

It's hard to distinguish her features, against the light. But her eyes gleam with an unusual brightness.

Behind her, stiff as a post, and black, is the silhouette of d'Arlon.

'Jeanne,' says the latter, 'you recognise these gentlemen, I believe?'

'But of course,' replies a hardly discernible voice.

I bow. Triel bows. Mme. d'Arlon offers us an icy hand.

The hanged man in our midst seems to be waiting to be presented in turn.

We exchange frightful banalities, which ring false.

D'Arlon climbs on to a table and starts to cut the rope holding the unfortunate Gérapin. Mme. d'Arlon keeps her eyes fixed on the

27

folded jacket on a chair, with a rose button-hole.

'By the way,' asks Triel, 'what was it you were trying to tell me?'

'I don't remember,' I say.

Triel doesn't insist and offers a hand to d'Arlon.

I step away, and—in a purely mechanical reaction, I swear—light a cigarette.

One puff, two puffs….

Benoît Gérapin, unhooked, is now stretched out on the table.

The smell of tobacco fills the shack.

Triel looks at me.

Mme. d'Arlon hasn't diverted her eyes.

CHAPTER IV

Conversation at twilight

The sun has gone down. The sky is like wounded flesh, with violet bruises and touches of pinkness.

Down here, in the greyness, everything has calmed down. On the surface, at least.

The comings and goings between the cabin, the manor, and the concierge's lodge are over.

The hanged man has been taken to the Fougeras' lodge. The doctor has come to certify the death. A police inspector, accompanied by d'Arlon, is conducting routine investigations.

I'm sitting next to Triel in the drawing room of the manor, on the first floor. Opposite us is Mme. d'Arlon... Mme. d'Arlon, our hostess.

She's talking. Everything she says is very simple, very plausible. For now, the drama seems a long way off....

Why must night fall during this time, so that imponderable amounts of shadow add to and affect the young woman's story?

She speaks in a low voice, even though there are no other ears to overhear us. Her eyes, fixed on the floor, avoid contact. The scene must look like an interrogation... And yet it was she who invited us here.

Mechanically, I follow her eyes and the movement of her lips. Does she use lipstick? I don't know.

I need to make an effort to pay attention to her words.

What is she saying?

Ah, yes, the park, the solitude... She describes her anxious adolescence, in this dilapidated manor. She has all the hesitations and delays of a woman undressing in front of a doctor. She lived alone with her mother, apparently. Her two brothers were killed in the war.

'My father died when I was very young....'

She lifts her eyes automatically towards a portrait we can't see.

'I was never very happy here, you know. So alone... And we were poor as well.'

The night casts its veil over the stains and mildew of the large drawing room.

'My mother would have died sooner than lose any part of the estate.

'And I think most of her fortune disappeared after the war due to bad investments by the family solicitor.

'As for me, I was just a bored little girl. Visitors were rare at Nanteuil. A few old folk from the region, now long gone.

'Our only company was the concierge's family, which you know about—the nephew, poor Benoît, and the daughter, Élise, who was my childhood companion, and who left the area when I myself did, to get married.

'How long the days were! And how silent the nights!'

There was a pause in the narrative, a sort of hesitation, perhaps calculated. Then a confession.

'I wasn't bored: I was afraid.

'Yes, as a child, I was always afraid, just as other children are always cold.'

There's sincerity in that voice.

'My mother, my mother whom I loved so much, always seemed anxious, on guard against I didn't know what....'

Despite myself, my attention wanders from her story. My eyes linger on the great park, now completely black, as seen through the glass of the windows. Only the crests of the trees can be seen against the grey sky. In such a way that, now, the park seems like a wall built to keep us in.

And yet, I couldn't have known that, all around us, at that very moment, invisible bolts were being shot.

A new name strikes my ear in Mme. d'Arlon's narrative: René. Who's this?

Ah, yes, her husband.

'We're relatives, you know, but very distant. He belongs to a branch of my family that took up residence in Indochina. In his childhood, he spent several vacations here in Nanteuil. He got on well with my brothers. And with me, too. We were good playmates.

'And then... Then we got to like each other more.

'We corresponded regularly. We got engaged like that, by letter, and without having seen each other for three years.

'The marriage was my mother's wish. She was thinking of my future. She worried about me remaining alone in this isolated manor.

'They were an excellent family, and rich, the d'Arlons.

'I remember seeing Lucien d'Arlon's beard when I was very young. He was René's father, who died there in 1915. He looked like a missionary. He was the administrator of the Kay coalmines, which he had helped to create. René succeeded him as head of the enterprise.'

Why, by the way, did this young woman feel it necessary to recount her entire life to two strangers?

'It was agreed that René would spend his next vacation in France. And that's when we would get married.

'And then, within a few days, my mother died.

'I was left alone here, with no friends and no family.

'So I left. I went to join my fiancé at the other end of the world. I couldn't wait for him all alone here for another year.

'I was welcomed there by René's family, and, three months later, I became his wife.

'For me, it was—at last—rest and security.

'It seemed to me that I was just starting to live. Then, I had to come back, less than a year after I'd left.

'It was René's wish. Naturally, he liked Nanteuil, the Nanteuil he scarcely knew, but which now belonged to him. He talked about it in his dreams, during those humid nights in Saigon!

'Our first quarrels occurred on that subject .

'Moreover, I must tell you, we were getting bizarre letters from Old Fougeras. Obscure and disquieting letters, in which he solicited, whilst not wishing to make it too obvious, the return of his masters. It became an obsession.

'René insisted… And I gave in.

'The lights back there went out, like chandeliers after a party. We arrived here one Sunday evening, as cold as a mid-winter night, in a hired car.

'And the gate had scarcely closed behind us *when it started again.*'

'What started again, madam?'

'The flights of the black birds… My baseless anxieties.

'I was so on edge I cried all night.

'What could I do? Whom could I lean on?

'My husband? You don't know him. He loves me, I know. But he doesn't like what he calls my childishness. He's an important man, a captain of industry.

'The police? What would I have said to the police?

'That's when I thought of you.'

'In what way?'

'To tell the truth, I'd thought about it already, on the boat, although more vaguely. There was a passenger—what was his name?—a tall man with hollow cheeks, who spoke about you, gentlemen. About a strange case you managed to solve, the two of you, in a little village on the Somme.

'The analogy of the situation struck me forcefully. In my distress, I resolved to call for your help.

'But what to say to my husband?

'For the first time, I lied to him. I made you imaginary childhood friends. And I spoke to him with such conviction that it was René who suggested I invite you, in the hope of taking my mind off other things.

'He found your address by phoning your newspaper. And, being the man of action that he is, I had to write out immediately, in front of him, the letter which you received.

'I was sitting at the little table, over there by the window, in the anxiety of the growing darkness. I was planning to go and explain everything to you the following day, under the pretext of a shopping trip to Paris.

'But the next day I had other worries on my mind. It was on the next day that....

'But I was telling you about the evening I wrote you the letter.'

'That's to say, yesterday evening.'

'That's right. My God, how long the hours have been since then....

'It was around five o'clock. My husband was about to go out. He offered to post it before the last collection.

'Left alone, I opened a book, but couldn't bring myself to read it. At eight o'clock, René returned. A few moments later, Josephine, the cook, served dinner. At almost the same time, Marthe Fougeras, the concierge, came in. She was surprised not to have seen her nephew. His dinner was getting cold... She wanted to know if we'd given Benoît some work to do.

'My husband replied that we hadn't seen Benoît at all that day.

'As a result of that simple incident, I couldn't eat. I slept badly.

'The following day—that's to say this morning— Benoît still hadn't turned up....'

Jeanne d'Arlon had to stop for a moment, out of breath. Her speech had become nervous and hurried.

'At around ten o'clock this morning, Marthe Fougeras learnt that Benoît had had a rendezvous the day before with one of his friends. He hadn't turned up.

'It was confirmed that Benoît hadn't been seen the previous evening, either in Bougival or Marly. *He seemed to have stayed inside the park.*

'The searches started. At noon, my husband asked that Paris send a police inspector. It was he who arrived a short while ago. From the drawing room and my bedroom, I heard the two Fougeras calling out willy-nilly.

'Whilst all that was going on, I'd forgotten all about the crazy initiative I'd taken in inviting you here. I only remembered your existence when I saw you just now, next to....'

She dared not continue.

'Next to the corpse, yes,' said Triel, completing the sentence.

There was a long silence.

'All in all, madam,' said Triel, 'our business here is over before it's started.'

The young woman made a gesture of excuse.

'All that remains,' continued Triel, 'is for us to take our leave.'

'Believe me, I'm sorry for the inconvenience I've caused.'

'Madam,' said Triel. 'We've only known you for a few moments, but those moments are such that we feel we've shared part of your existence.

'And, as for the title of friend, which you bestowed with subterfuge, I believe we have now earned it.'

'I believe so, too,' replied Jeanne d'Arlon.

I strived anxiously to discern the degree of sincerity in all those words.

'Madam,' said Triel, 'you've lived for a long time under the threat of a tragedy.

'That tragedy has now, alas, occurred.

'I believe that now your ordeals are over and the black birds, as you call them, will now fly away.'

Jeanne d'Arlon spread out her hands.

'Does one ever know?' she said.

The darkness completely prevented seeing her expression.

Triel hesitated. He decided brusquely:

'I have some other questions I'd like to ask you, madam. If I do, will you answer?'

'Ask your questions.'

'Monsieur d'Arlon has just returned,' I said.

Through the window, I could dimly perceive the lord of the manor advancing through the half-light, accompanied by a stranger.

'Not a word in front of him,' implored the young woman.

'We still have two minutes,' said Triel. 'Answer succinctly, madam.

'You've stressed the fear that this estate has always inspired in your mother and yourself.

'Very impressive, all that.

'But what lies at the origin of those fears? Real threats? A tradition?'

'Nothing,' replied Jeanne d'Arlon.

'Not an omen, not an act, not a noise. Nothing. Nothing, truth be told!'

Triel clicked his tongue.

'That's not much,' he said.

'Did you have any enemies?'

'Who would hate two solitary women?'

'Who knows? The worst enemies are the oldest ones, generally.'

'We didn't have any friends,' said the young woman.

Triel considered a question, but didn't pose it, asking simply:

'What was your personal relationship with Benoît Gérapin?'

'Benoît Gérapin was the gardener of the estate and general handyman.'

We heard the stairs creaking under d'Arlon's footsteps.

'Has anyone else lived here, near you?'

'René d'Arlon, when he was a student, during summer breaks… Élise Fougeras, the concierge's daughter, whom I already told you about.'

CHAPTER V

Inspector Troubert

The door opened.

'It's pitch dark in here,' said d'Arlon's voice.

'Please go in, my dear sir.'

At the same time, he stepped back and turned on the electric switch. The light caused us to blink. Mme. d'Arlon turned her head away.

'Allow me to present Inspector Troubert, who has come to investigate the unfortunate accident.'

Inspector Troubert raised an old boater in acknowledgement. Reflexively, he wiped his feet on the carpet as if it were a doormat. He looked like one of those poor devils you see roaming the racetracks after having lost their last centime. It was only through the passage of time that we discerned, under that ragged exterior, a dangerous perspicacity and a total contempt for danger.

Having wiped his feet, and still in the doorway, he bowed ceremoniously.

D'Arlon made the introductions from a distance:

'Our friends, M. Dutheil, M. Triel.'

A gleam appeared beneath Troubert's bushy eyebrows. Perhaps our names sounded vaguely familiar. He already sensed illegal competition.

He finally stepped into the room.

'Honoured, gentlemen, I'm sure.'

He coughed.

'So… are these gentlemen interested in this matter?'

'These gentlemen are my friends,' repeated d'Arlon. 'By an unfortunate coincidence, they happened to arrive at the very moment the tragedy plunged us into grief.'

'Unfortunate coincidence, indeed… A sad thing, is it not, gentlemen?

'And have you been designated to help?'

'We arrived at Bougival on the half-past five tram,' said Triel. 'We found the body at the same time as M. d'Arlon, guided by the cries of the concierge.

'A sad sight, indeed!'

Troubert noted, in Triel's apparent willingness to oblige, a desire to limit his investigation. He put up his moral antennae, felt the resistance, and withdrew into his shell.

'Very well!' he said. 'Very well! I knew there were two guests in the manor... But I hadn't realised it was you....

'Oh, I beg your pardon, madam!'

Troubert discovered Mme. d'Arlon, and his eyes gleamed again. A strange fellow, this one. I thought of those pictures of signal boxes where the lights come on automatically.

'Upon my word!' said d'Arlon. 'This is my wife, whom I hadn't noticed. Anyone would think you were hiding, Jeanne.'

Troubert studied the young woman with an almost loving interest. Then he chose an armchair from which he could observe us all.

At exactly the same moment, Mme. d'Arlon stood up, as if she were at the other end of a see-saw:

'Excuse me, gentlemen, but I'm exhausted... I'm going to get some sleep.'

'Madam,' said Troubert at once, 'I must ask you to make the necessary effort to stay with us for a few moments more. Your testimony is precious to me.'

He pulled a well-worn notebook out of his pocket, and winked amicably in our direction.

'This tragedy we all regret,' he said, his face beaming, 'is a suicide, a sad suicide.

'But I'm obliged to make a report.

'What can I say? We police are civil servants, just like everybody.'

'Stay, Jeanne,' said d'Arlon.

The young woman sat down again in her armchair.

Troubert placed his boater on the table, stretched out in the armchair, and crossed his legs.

D'Arlon, who could hardly be pleased by such behaviour, started to wrinkle his nose.

'I've already been asking around,' said Troubert, tugging at his moustache. 'That's how I know how Benoît Gérapin spent the time yesterday, up until seven fifty-five precisely.

'Here's the first curious thing: during that whole time, nothing unusual is revealed. Absolutely nothing!'

He looked at us with an air of satisfaction.

'Here's an interesting detail: do you know where Gérapin was supposed to spend yesterday evening? No?

'Madam?'

'How should I know?' said Mme. d'Arlon.

'Well, he was supposed to go to the Casino de Paris! That's pretty odd, isn't it, for a candidate for suicide?

'He already had a reservation. He had a rendezvous arranged with his friend Robert Flambaire at the bridge in Bougival.

'At six fifty-five, returning from the *Café de la Mairie,* where he'd partaken of aperitifs with a couple of market gardeners, he banged on Flambaire's door and shouted:

'"See you in a little while. Try not to make us late!"

'The poor lad had a loud voice. Half a dozen people heard him. Flambaire, from his window on the first floor, said he looked jaunty and had his cap over his ear, as usual.

'A little later, the wife of an associate crossed him in the street, hurrying, almost running, towards the manor. And a workman returning to la Celle-Saint-Cloud was overtaken by him, and saw him, from a distance, go through the Nanteuil gate.

'So, from the café to the park here, no notable encounters, certainly nothing to suggest Gérapin was harbouring any fatal intention.

'The decisive factor is not to be found outside the manor.'

Troubert nodded his head sadly and repeated:

'The decisive factor is not to be found *outside* the manor.'

He'd taken his cigarette case out of his pocket. He put it back after looking at it vaguely, forgetting to help himself.

'So Gérapin comes through the Nanteuil gate. He goes into his relatives' lodge, asking them to prepare "something to eat, and quickly."

'Then he goes out into the park.

'What was he going to do in that park at nightfall, I hear you ask?

'Well, he was going to hang himself!

'Half an hour later—the medical examiner confirms this—he was hanging at the end of a rope. He still had the ticket for the Casino de Paris in his wallet. And, in his button-hole, the wild rose plucked from his aunt's garden.

'His soup was getting cold in the bowl. His friend Flambaire was pacing up and down on the bridge at Bougival....'

For the second time, Jeanne d'Arlon got up. She was certainly whiter than the paper of the notebook in which Troubert was languidly waiting to record the depositions.

She made a gesture to indicate she couldn't take any more. She left.

D'Arlon made no attempt to stop her, and Troubert, his melodramatic effects cut short, sat with his mouth open, trying to think of something to say.

*****

The endurance test Troubert had tried to impose had been cut short. Facing the inspector, there remained only three men, not disposed to let him lord it over them.

Troubert, unhappy, chewed on his moustache. He gave up telling stories and became brief and brusque.

'So,' he said, 'as I was saying, Gérapin's death can be placed between seven o'clock and seven thirty. Therefore, my report has to cover the movements of everyone on the estate over that time period.

'A simple formality, you'll agree.'

He brandished his notebook. A number of greasy papers fell out, which he carefully collected.

'I'm not going talk about the Fougeras. They were in their lodge, in the company of an aged neighbour, deaf and frail, but not blind.

'As for you, gentlemen....'

He turned towards Triel and me. Was he serious, or was he just pretending?

'We were in Paris,' said Triel.

'That's true. You already told me that.

'In fact, gentlemen, because you are the first witnesses, please give me your address.'

Which is what we did.

Troubert turned a few degrees in his seat.

'Monsieur d'Arlon was absent, I believe?'

'I left by car at around six o'clock, on various errands,' replied d'Arlon. 'Émile was driving.'

'From seven o'clock to a quarter to eight, I was with M. Leclément, discussing masonry work. I was giving him instructions for the renovation of the manor, which is falling in ruins.

'At what time did we return to the manor? Probably around eight o'clock. The servants, or the Fougeras, can give you a more precise time.

'I went up to my bedroom to clean up: five minutes at most.

'Then I went to the dining room.

'That's it.'

'Was Mme. d'Arlon waiting for you there?'

'She joined me almost immediately.'

'Where was she before that?'

'I've no idea. In the drawing room, I suppose, or in the park.'

The inspector made a gesture indicating that was all perfectly natural.

Then he asked:

'Will you allow me to pose the same questions to your wife?'

'Not now!' said d'Arlon, without hesitation.

'And yet....'

'It's completely pointless. Mme. d'Arlon is indisposed. I can't see how it can be of any interest to you to know whether she was reading a book by Henry Bordeaux twenty-four hours ago, or watching lilacs grow.'

Troubert wanted to overcome this obstacle, or get around it.

He was looking for the right tactic when d'Arlon, going on the attack, pushed him rashly.

'First of all, I can't see where your questions are leading, if you'll permit me to say so. Gérapin's death is the result of a suicide. That's been accepted, hasn't it?

'So?'

Troubert nodded his head and weighed his words carefully.

'Of course it's a suicide,' he replied.

'But it's a very odd one.'

CHAPTER VI

The manor empties

'I don't see what's particularly odd about this suicide,' said d'Arlon.

'Ah,' sighed the inspector, 'you have so little experience in this kind of crime. It practically rains suicides. They are generally the result of amorous collisions, if I may put it that way. Lovers' encounters are, however, less violent than rapid encounters. Those are far more murderous!

'But I can't see whom Benoît Gérapin could have clashed with in such a fashion. Because he was alone in the park.'

No one said a word.

Troubert continued calmly:

'As well as the violent, there are also the depressed, the oppressed and the tormented. But, strictly between us, Gérapin didn't belong in any of those categories.

'The *Bistro de la Poste* told me some spicy stories about him. He was quite a lad, that Benoît. The local Casanova. Always a song on his lips. And balcony seats at the Casino de Paris.

'It even seems, according to the parents and the neighbours, that he was particularly happy recently, during the days preceding your arrival.'

'Really?' said d'Arlon grudgingly.

'Yes. Those are the prior events, Monsieur d'Arlon, which make the whole business rather peculiar.

'Let me be clear. At this very moment, tongues are wagging in the village.

'It's in all our interests to shine a light on this story, if only to clip their tongues.'

D'Arlon wiped his brow.

Clearly, he was desperate to terminate the discussion. But he felt the very real menace represented by the inspector.

Why this suicide? The whole region will be repeating the question tomorrow. And where will the insinuations stop?

'There are things you don't know,' murmured d'Arlon.

'Oh, really?' said Troubert, the automatic gleam reappearing in his eyes.

'These gentlemen,' said d'Arlon, turning towards us, 'these gentlemen, who've known Nanteuil a long time, know what I'm about to say.'

We knew, obviously, but only very recently!

'It's certain,' I said, 'that the property has acquired a disturbing reputation.'

'Oh, really?' repeated the inspector.

I didn't proceed any further, prudently leaving the word to d'Arlon.

He was no doubt repulsed by the thought of revealing the internal affairs of Nanteuil to such a scruffy policeman, but he resigned himself to the task.

And he repeated the narrative we had just heard from his wife's lips.

From time to time, Triel or I confirmed one detail or another of his account.

Troubert looked at the three of us in turn.

'All those,' he said crudely, 'are just stories.'

'Really?' said d'Arlon furiously. 'Well then, just wait a second.'

He left the room. We heard two doors slam.

'What's he gone to look for?' mused Troubert.

D'Arlon returned almost immediately. He was carrying a wooden chest under his arm. He took out three stacks of letters and threw the first on the table in front of us.

'I authorise you to read them.'

We brought our chairs closer.

D'Arlon remained standing, arms folded.

'What are these?' asked Troubert.

'Letters my fiancée sent me from Nanteuil to Saigon.

'You came here to investigate. Here are some documents. Read them. Consult them.'

I was a bit uneasy—wrongly so—about the idea of reading love letters.

The tender feelings they contained hardly matched those of the serials in the popular magazines. Mlle. de Nanteuil revealed herself to be melancholic by nature. Boredom and anxiety were her two principal themes, but there was a striking lack of specifics.

The phrase: "I'll explain when I see you," came up often.

'And when your fiancée did eventually see you,' said Triel, 'did she explain?'

'No. Nothing.'

'So what did you think of all that?'

'I didn't pay it any attention.

'Young girls fret and sigh for reasons even they don't understand.'

'Yes. You thought that marriage would be the best remedy.'

'Only the facts didn't confirm your expectations.'

'Judge for yourself,' replied d'Arlon, untying the second package.

'These are the letters my wife wrote me from Saigon, when I was on assignment to the Kay coalmines, shortly before our return.'

There was no doubt that marriage had humanised the young woman. The tone of the correspondence was more personal. But there were no little secrets of a young wife. There was only insistent discussion about the return to France.

Asked by her husband to reserve places on the liner, Mme. d'Arlon hedged and played for time.

D'Arlon's replies were not included in the correspondence. But one could infer an imperious tone, to judge by the reactions of the young woman.

'Family quarrels,' concluded Troubert.

As if playing his trump card, d'Arlon threw the third package down.

This time, the writing paper was cheap, the handwriting clumsy, and the spelling unorthodox.

Troubert read at random, in a low voice:

"About what's going on here, it could be better, the lettuces are good, but we would like it better if Monsieur and Madame were here to see what's happening, which might not be anything…"

'The famous letters from Old Fougeras?'

'Yes.'

All the letters—about twenty in all—were from the same pen, and mixed reports about the vegetables with discreet complaints about ill-defined matters.

'I'll ask the author a few questions later on,' said Troubert.

'But my mind, my poor Monsieur d'Arlon, is already made up.

43

'There are a lot of omissions in these letters, but not an ounce of mystery!

'There are two contradictory themes running throughout the correspondence, which can be summarised succinctly:

'The Fougeras theme—perhaps I should call it the Gérapin-Fougeras theme, which urges you and your wife to return to Nanteuil.

'The Jeanne d'Arlon theme—if I may be permitted to call it that—which is the exact opposite.

'Mme. d'Arlon has no desire—absolutely none!—to see the good people who miss her so much.

'She sensed that her return alongside you would lead to tragedy. Her whole attitude proves it!'

Triel continued to examine the letters strewn across the table.

D'Arlon, his head down and the veins in his temple throbbing, was listening to the inspector. The atmosphere was becoming tense.

'It's precisely this intuition which is the most puzzling element of this whole business.

'It's not a police matter, obviously. It's a—how to put it?—psychological problem. Yes, that's it: psychological. The whole affair is being played out inside people's heads… and hearts.'

This last statement had gone a bit too far in terms of insinuation.

If Troubert had been looking to create a stir, he'd succeeded.

D'Arlon looked up, seething with anger.

'Tell me, then,' he asked brutally. 'If it's not a police problem, then what precisely are you doing here?'

'Me? I'm enormously interested in psychology,' replied Troubert.

For a whole minute D'Arlon asked himself silently whether he should grab this tramp from the *Sûreté* by the scruff of his neck and throw him out.

He chose a solution more appropriate to the situation in which we found ourselves.

He grabbed the bell rope hanging on the wall and tugged it violently.

Whose coat was he going to ask for? Troubert's, or all of ours?

Elementary courtesy demanded that we all leave. But a burning curiosity held us all there.

D'Arlon tugged at the rope a second time. No one answered.

It was obviously not his day.

Troubert, his head buried in his shoulders and his eyes half-closed, stared at the floor between parted knees.

Triel, crossing his own legs, stared thoughtfully at the chandelier.

'Josephine! Josephine!'

D'Arlon, standing in the doorway, shouted at the top of his voice. No Josephine.

Had Josephine gone to hang herself as well?

'Marie!'

Troubert pulled a face for my benefit and, without changing his position of sleeping vulture, observed:

'The ladies are in no hurry to come here.'

Triel, abandoning his contemplation of the chandelier, started to squint in the direction of the corridor.

A rustling of skirts could be heard. But it was neither Josephine nor Marie. It was Mme. d'Arlon.

'At last!' exclaimed d'Arlon. 'Can you please tell me what's happened to those women? Where's Marie?'

'You know very well that the cleaning lady leaves at six o'clock. Marie's gone home.'

'Very well, but where's Josephine?'

'Josephine has gone as well.'

'What?'

'She gave notice just now. She won't stay overnight in this manor at any price, in proximity to a hanged man.'

'And you let her go?'

'Should I have tied her to the stove?'

'Perfect! Perfect!'

'The Fougeras are mourning their nephew, so there's no question of asking them to do the cooking.

'So we're alone here. Charming!

'But... you as well, Jeanne?'

D'Arlon noticed that his wife had changed her clothes. She was now wearing a black and white chequered suit.

'Are you leaving as well?'

'Surely you're not planning for us to stay here alone tonight?' replied the young woman.

'You could have asked me my intentions, instead of notifying me of yours.

'I don't appreciate my behaviour being governed by that of my subordinates.'

'René, we *mustn't* stay here tonight.'

'Jeanne, I fear this suicide has addled your mind.'

Triel stood up, and I followed suit.

'Madam,' said Triel, 'we have no wish to add to all your worries. Please allow us to take our leave.'

Troubert, much against his will, stood up in turn.

'Gentlemen,' said Jeanne d'Arlon calmly, 'we are immensely grateful to you for having helped us in these trying times.

'We'll drive you back to Paris.'

She turned to look at her husband.

'I wish to go out tonight.'

D'Arlon didn't say a word, but his stare, fixed on us, said:

'You can clear off right away.'

Truly, manor life can have its awkward moments, as I had only just begun to realise.

Troubert, Triel and I stood motionless, lined up behind one another.

After several interminable minutes, d'Arlon said, with a forced smile:

'I yield to the unanimity of my wife, my guests, and my cook. Let's go.'

He added:

'Excuse me a moment.

'I need to check whether or not my chauffeur has also left us.'

He bowed slightly, turned on his heels, and disappeared into the corridor.

Mme. d'Arlon avoided looking at us.

She carefully sorted out all the letters on the table, placed them back in the chest, and placed the chest on one of the shelves.

Troubert watched the young woman out of the corner of his eye.

I pulled Triel over to one of the windows.

'What's she running from?' I murmured.

'Her husband? Her remorse?'

Triel shrugged in ignorance.

'Or perhaps that vague menace we've sensed from time to time?'

From the darkness of the park came the sound of a car horn.

CHAPTER VII

The closed gate

In the game that was being played, it was easy to delude ourselves that we were the players. Nothing of the sort: we were the ball.

One swipe of the racket had driven us out of the manor. But already, at the other end of the court, another racket was beginning its swing....

For now, six of us were packed into d'Arlon's 10CV, which looked like one of those marauding taxis which compete with the suburban trams.

'All present?' asked d'Arlon, climbing in beside the chauffeur.

'Present and correct.'

We were leaving, we had left....

The manor, henceforth deserted, had disappeared behind us.

It was an escape, of course, but a slow, dignified escape. The great black park surrounding us murmured confused and wild things. But we no longer cared what the park thought.

After one final turn, the monumental gate appeared suddenly in the headlights. The chauffeur cut the motor and the car's momentum carried it forward. We watched the gate approach and grow larger, as if in a motion picture.

Five metres away, the chauffeur stopped the vehicle and turned his inscrutable yellow face towards d'Arlon.

'Shall I get out and open it?'

'That's the concierge's job,' replied d'Arlon. 'Besides, he's probably locked it.'

The concierge's lodge was only discernible from the feeble light coming through the shutters: the light from a funeral wake.

'Well, Émile?'

The chauffeur honked his horn in the silence, like the first shot across an obstacle.

A two-minute wait. Then an illuminated rectangle appeared on the side wall of the lodge. Old Fougeras emerged and approached the vehicle.

It was the first time I'd seen the man. His back was bent and he walked slightly crab-wise, with that clumsy agility one sees in a daddy-long-legs. Excessively long arms and legs contributed to the impression. Despite the coolness of the night, he was only wearing a shirt and trousers.

D'Arlon leant out of the window.

'Listen. We're not going to spend the night here. I'll be back tomorrow, in the morning.'

Old Fougeras bent a little more, turned on his heel, and hastened towards the gate without saying a word.

He went through the usual motions: inserted the key in the lock, pushed on the knob, and pulled the heavy door towards him.

Émile revved the engine, which responded with a series of purrs.

Only the gate didn't open.

*****

Pantomime under an electric moonlight….

Old Fougeras, upset, thrust his long arms through the bars. A shadow ten metres long reproduced his gestures.

We sat motionless, our backs pressed to the cushions. We didn't realise immediately that we were well and truly imprisoned in Nanteuil.

A rapid movement, followed by the crisp slam of a door, broke the charm. Triel had just jumped out of the car and was running towards the gate.

Émile took his foot off the accelerator. Jeanne d'Arlon, who was dreaming about who-knows-what, came to herself and fluttered her eyelids.

Two minutes later, we had all joined Triel.

'It's always been a bit hard to move,' said Old Fougeras… 'But never like tonight.'

Impatient hands pushed his away from the knob and tried themselves. The knob didn't move.

'The keyhole is scratched,' said Triel.

'It's always been a bit hard, particularly when it's wet,' repeated Old Fougeras, 'but never like tonight.

'Because tonight, well....'

A hip bumped me out of the way. Troubert, aware of the gravity of the situation, was pushing everyone aside.

He stood squarely in front of the recalcitrant gate, and tried to manoeuvre the knob gently. Then he lit a match.

For as long as the flame burned, the inspector, bent in two, dug into the interior of the lock with a pen-knife.

'What's that?' he asked loudly.

'Sand?'

He lit a second match. D'Arlon leaned over as well:

'It's sand, all right.

'Someone forced gravel into the mechanism, don't you think? And forcefully.

'With the help of a lever,' d'Arlon concluded. 'Do you see that scratch on the paintwork? That's the fulcrum of the lever.'

In the ensuing silence, footsteps could be heard approaching.

Troubert turned round, rather too nervously.

It was Triel rejoining the group.

'Did you go for a walk?' asked the inspector.

'Yes, I've just been to look at the side door.'

'Sapristi!' exclaimed d'Arlon, punching one hand with the other. 'It's true... The little door! And so?'

'Locked,' replied Triel laconically.

'Sh—!' exclaimed Troubert, letting go of the end of the match.

Was it just because he'd burnt his fingertips? His face was now hidden in shadow.

Interjections were flying between us. D'Arlon's voice dominated, an angry, commanding voice.

'Fougeras, where are you?'

'Here. I'm here, sir.'

'I can't see you. Come closer... More!'

'So, what do you think of all this?'

'Of... of what, sir?'

D'Arlon contained himself.

'The gate. The door that can't be opened.'

'Generally,' stammered the old man, 'when it rains—.'

'Be quiet!' shouted d'Arlon.

The old man waved his long arms in a desperate display of sign

49

language.

'Let's see,' asked Troubert more gently, 'when did you open the gate for the first time?'

'I—I don't know, sir.'

D'Arlon sighed in exasperation.

'When your master's car comes in or goes out,' continued the inspector patiently, 'you open the gate, don't you?'

'Yes, sir.'

'When did the car come in for the last time?'

'Last night,' said d'Arlon.

'Last night,' repeated Old Fougeras.

'So you did indeed open the gate last night?'

'Yes, sir.'

'And since?'

'Since?'

'Yes, since last night have you touched the gate?'

'No, sir.'

'At that time, did you find the gate particularly hard to move?'

'No, sir.

'But it wasn't as wet.'

'Twenty-four hours,' murmured Troubert, 'is obviously plenty of time to sabotage the lock.

'But what about the small door?

'When did you lock the small door, Fougeras?'

'When Josephine Trémélanier left, just now. I locked it behind her.'

'That's less than half an hour ago,' said Troubert.

'About half an hour ago,' said Mme. d'Arlon.

'This is like pulling teeth,' exclaimed Troubert, throwing up his arms. 'In half an hour, someone knew… someone was able…

'Joséphine Trémélanier can be sure to get a visit from me early tomorrow morning—whether she's in bed or not!'

'Since Joséphine Trémélanier left,' asked d'Arlon, 'did you see anyone approaching the gate? Or someone roaming around?'

'I don't know. I didn't stay to watch.'

'Of course. But you didn't hear any suspicious noises?'

'No, sir.'

'How's that for servants you can trust!' exploded d'Arlon. 'Blind and deaf! Locks get broken under their noses, and they see nothing and hear nothing!'

'René,' interceded Mme. d'Arlon.

She nodded towards the little lodge, where the light from the wake was filtering through the shutters.

'Thank you,' said d'Arlon to Old Fougeras. 'You may go.'

And, when the other looked at him in bewilderment:

'Return to your lodge, and don't leave!'

Old Fougeras left, his back more bent than when he came, and his walk more crab-like than before.

We went as a group to the secondary door. It was made of oak, with iron fittings. We patted the walls. They were three metres high!

Troubert clicked his tongue, with a sort of professional respect.

'It's solid,' he said, 'really solid.'

I went back to Jeanne d'Arlon, silent and alone. She had not come with us. She seemed not to want to approach the concierge's lodge.

'I fear, madam,' I said, 'that we shall be your guests tonight.'

'Yes,' she said. 'It's awful.'

'You're too kind,' I said, jokingly.

'Oh, you know very well what I mean. What's awful is being trapped here... Why would anyone do that? And what are they preparing at this very moment?'

D'Arlon's raised voice could be heard again.

'Hey, over there! Monsieur Dutheil!'

I turned round.

'Gentlemen, the question is this: Are we going to stand here, all six of us, and admit we can't shift a piece of old iron?

'Six people working together can shift anything!'

'We could always try,' said Troubert, without bothering to hide his scepticism.

We grabbed hold of the bars.

D'Arlon gave the command:

'Heave... ho!'

Nothing.

The second effort was more violent. The gate shuddered slightly.

'It has to break,' said d'Arlon, in a sort of cold exultation, 'or tell us why not.'

He took off his hat and threw it on the ground. I reacted by taking off my jacket.

'Heave… ho!'

The gate didn't break or tell us why not. Anyone would have thought it was rooted to the ground. There were another half-a-dozen tries, at the end of which everyone was upset and pulling in all directions.

Troubert was the first to break it off:

'It's not worth killing ourselves.'

'Let go, madam, please,' I said.

I had to prise Jeanne d'Arlon's frail fingers loose from the bars.

The face she turned towards me was that of a wounded woman. In the glare of the headlights, her cheeks and hair looked white.

"She's a prisoner," I told myself as we exchanged looks, "a prisoner who's afraid to let go of the bars of her cell.

"Can she already hear steps resonating in the corridor?"

'Whoever locked us in,' said d'Arlon, 'is watching us from the other side of the gate and having a great time!'

'Whoever locked us in,' said Troubert, 'stayed on the same side with us.'

Jeanne d'Arlon couldn't suppress a moan.

Her husband turned to the inspector.

'Why do you say that?'

'Just an impression. Otherwise this comedy would make no sense.'

'You're very lucky,' said d'Arlon, 'if you can see the possibility of any sense in this comedy.

'All I can see is an idiotic joke.

'But Jeanne….'

He noticed his wife, her face deathly pale, clinging to my arm.

He took her from me, with a savage tenderness which surprised me.

'Excuse me, my darling… I'm neglecting you, aren't I? And you're cold…

'Shall we go inside?'

'Madam,' interjected Troubert. 'Madam, a word, if you will.

'This is your home. You grew up in this park. You must know every nook and cranny.

'What is the length of the perimeter of the Nanteuil park?'

'Approximately three thousand metres,' replied d'Arlon.

'And is there, anywhere along the three thousand metres perimeter, a spot where the wall is dilapidated to the point someone could climb over?

'Madam, I'm calling on your knowledge of the premises.'

'Alas, no,' replied Jeanne d'Arlon. 'The walls were constantly being repaired, rebuilt, even heightened in some places. All the trees which could have facilitated a climb were cut down.

'It was my mother who supervised all such work. She was obsessed with security. Anyone would have thought she feared a danger.'

'That's correct,' said d'Arlon. 'It's that poor woman who's trapped us here, in a way.'

'It's impossible for there not to be other doors anywhere else along the perimeter,' observed Triel.

'Well, Jeanne?' urged d'Arlon.

The young woman hesitated.

'I know there are three little doors,' she said eventually, 'but....'

'But?'

'But they're just like this service door. So....'

'So there's a good chance they've been locked in the same way.'

'That remains to be seen,' said d'Arlon.

'That's already been seen,' growled Troubert.

'Those doors are a long way away, René,' said the young woman. 'And it's a very dark night....'

'But, my dear,' replied d'Arlon, 'it's precisely because of you, and to please you, that we're acting out this grotesque farce. We're trying to avoid our own residence.

'We can go back, if you want. We can have dinner and go to bed. Tomorrow is another day!'

The young woman's lips trembled.

I intervened to stop the domestic dispute.

'I'm quite happy to do the reconnaissance of the three doors,' I volunteered, 'with my friend Triel at the wheel.'

'And who will guide you?' asked d'Arlon. 'Are you going to take my wife along with you?'

Goaded by my questioner, I was about to reply with some insult, when Troubert stepped in front of me and cut off the discussion.

Facing d'Arlon, he said:

'I'm not in favour of quarrelling amongst ourselves,' he said, 'and I speak from experience. Afterwards, it's the devil who picks up the pieces.

'Why don't we all go there together?'

'Why not, indeed?' said d'Arlon. 'The more madmen there are, the more laughter there is!'

*****

So it was that the 10CV started up for the second time, carrying— towards destinations less and less certain—its load of six people, a whole baggage of fears and worries, and not a few potential dissenters.

Troubert was the only one to find the adventure charming, or at least to pretend to.

The sight of the interior, with its blinds drawn, seemed to provoke mirth.

He leaned back in his seat to whisper in my ear:

'Anyone would think we were on our way to the Bois de Boulogne!'

Upset at the thought that Mme. d'Arlon might hear, I said nothing.

But Mme. d'Arlon herself appeared to be in a somnambulistic state, concentrating entirely on giving the chauffeur directions in a very indistinct voice:

'Keep to the right, Émile.'

'That reminds me,' continued Troubert impudently, 'of a story from around 1910. It was about an American woman—.'

'Be quiet,' I said. 'Can't you hear, all around us….'

There was nothing you could put your finger on, but… the glass in the windows was rattling… dead wood was snapping under the tyres…branches were brushing against the wings and the doors, and sometimes getting caught….

'Keep to the right again, Émile.'

I knew the paths were becoming narrower and less well maintained the farther we penetrated into the park. Nonetheless, there was a distinct impression that the park was tightening its grip on us, as if to seize us in its embrace.

'How much longer?' asked Troubert.

'We're almost there.'

We were arriving at a particularly muddy part of the park, and the wheels, too heavily loaded, were spinning. Émile was trying to compensate by using the accelerator and the gears. The resultant jolts threw us one against the other, and all the joints of the vehicle groaned at the same time.

All that to arrive at door number one, black against the white background of a wall, freshly replastered and as impregnable as a tombstone!

*****

Triel tried to scale the wall and failed.

Troubert shattered the lock with several shots from his revolver and prised it free from the oak door using the starting-handle of the car.

But, after all the metal had fallen into the mud, the door still didn't open.

'How about that?' said Troubert. 'Is it clamped on the other side, or walled up, or what?'

The scope of the attempts to thwart us was disconcerting.

Someone must have preceded us, going round the park and blocking all the exits. Someone very familiar with the layout of the estate.

'Émile, turn the car around,' said d'Arlon.

'It's pointless, is it not, for us repeat the experience with the other two doors?'

'Completely pointless,' agreed Triel.

The chauffeur managed, with great difficulty, to turn the car round in the undergrowth, despite the bushes and puddles.

He returned in front of our group and opened the door in true servant style.

D'Arlon deferred to his wife.

'After you.'

Mme. d'Arlon climbed into the car.

'Just like a condemned woman climbing into a tumbril,' Troubert whispered in my ear, no longer thinking of the Bois de Boulogne.

He climbed in behind her and I followed.

SECOND PART

CHAPTER I

The return

The return trip only lasted a quarter of an hour, but it was an awful quarter of an hour.

I shall gloss over the incidents which only appeared important because of our overwrought imaginations: a broken branch falling noisily on the roof of the car, Mme. d'Arlon failing to find the path home, Émile stalling the car in full view of a withered willow at the edge of a pool of darkness....

Each time, the emotion inside the car rose like the mercury in a thermometer under the armpit of a feverish patient.

When the manor finally loomed in front of us, shrouded in a light mist, someone let out a deep sigh of relief.

It was the refuge, the harbour....

A minute later, without anything new having happened, and purely due to our imaginations, we felt it had more the appearance of a trap.

Had all the obstacles we had faced been arranged with the unique goal of bringing us here?

Like game birds driven out by beaters, were we falling into a trap?

Émile was about to stop the car by the front steps.

Troubert called out to him.

'Ho, chauffeur! Drive once around the premises, would you? And slowly.'

Émile obeyed, stepped gently on the accelerator and turned.

Six pairs of eyes, with heightened attention, I can assure you, scrutinised every facet of the manor. We found nothing abnormal. Which didn't really prove anything.

The car returned to where it had started and everyone got out.

'Should I put the car in the garage, sir?' asked Émile, from behind us.

The garage was opposite the front face of the building.

'Leave it where it is,' replied d'Arlon.

The 10CV sat there like a shipwreck in the darkness which was closing around it.

D'Arlon retrieved the house key from his pocket. Troubert retrieved a gun from his.

On the sill of the corridor, we dispensed with the customary "After you" and "No, I insist, after you." We entered as we were, in a bunch. D'Arlon switched on the electricity, whilst Troubert shut the door behind us.

Was the wide corridor with its black and white tiles a trap?

Were the bench with the threadbare cover, the coat rack with several rags hanging from it, and the stove with the rusty pipe all snares?

The glass eyes of the hunting trophies on the walls gleamed dully.

And what would Freud have had to say about sadness of the empty umbrella stand?

Troubert advanced with a curious mixture of defiance and swagger, dragging the soles of his shoes over the tiles, his left hand in his pocket, but keeping the revolver in his right.

'I've cleaned trenches in my time,' he said. 'A corridor of stuffed stags' heads doesn't scare me.'

We followed him.

The doors were opened in all the rooms and the electricity switched on.

Triel verified that the bench, which was hollow, did not harbour a clandestine visitor.

From the dining room, I heard Troubert's raised voice in the drawing room.

'Something has changed here,' he was saying.

'I can't see what,' replied d'Arlon, who was with him.

'Mme. d'Arlon, if you please,' called the inspector.

We all rushed to the drawing room.

'Madam, it seems to me that, as we were leaving this room, you placed the small chest containing the letters M. d'Arlon had read out on that shelf.'

'That's correct.'

The shelf was empty, and the chest had disappeared.

'I was the last to leave the room,' I said. 'It was I who turned out the light. At that moment, the chest was still in its place.'

'So,' said d'Arlon, 'someone must have come in here whilst we were away.'

'Not necessarily,' said Triel. 'That someone could have been hiding.'

'And slipped away afterwards, using a duplicate key?'

'Not necessarily,' said Troubert. 'He may still be here.'

Frowning, he looked around.

'In any case, I promise you we're going to make sure.'

Through the windows, thanks to the layout of the trees in the park, the lights of Bougival could be seen.

Mme. d'Arlon noticed that I was looking at that manifestation of life outside.

'If we wanted to,' she said, 'we could attract attention.'

'How?' retorted d'Arlon. 'By calling out and firing a revolver in the air, I suppose? Or by lighting fires, like castaways on a desert island?'

I wanted to intervene, but he cut me off.

'All this because two or three old locks have become rusty due to the humidity. Five able-bodied men are afraid of being alone at night in a manor. A woman, that's understandable.

'Tomorrow morning, Old Fougeras will ask the first peasant who passes to fetch a locksmith. And it will all be over.'

'Tomorrow morning,' murmured Mme. d'Arlon, with a shiver.

I shivered as well.

I, too, felt as though I was at the entrance to a dark passage strewn with traps.

CHAPTER II

The bare hand

Troubert took charge. As searches go, this one was meticulous, and merits being described in detail, for several reasons.

The ground floor of the manor consisted of, on either side of a central corridor: to the right, in succession, drawing room-dining room-bedroom.

To the left, in succession, kitchen-laundry room.

Troubert adopted what he called the "rifleman's approach."

A first group, Triel-d'Arlon, would share the search of the right-hand side. Under orders from Troubert, they would start from the front façade wall and work their way towards the rear wall, searching each room in turn.

In the same way, a second group, Troubert- Émile, would take the left-hand side.

As for me, I was the centre of the system. Seated on a bench at one end of the corridor, near the entrance door, my mission was to watch the corridor and make sure that no one came out of the rooms being searched.

The intention was that, once both groups had completed their objectives, we could be certain that the terrain contained no suspicious element.

The groups would meet at the end of the corridor. From there a second expedition would be launched towards the cellar and a third towards the first floor.

Troubert had slipped his revolver into my hand. And, at the same time, he had whispered in my ear:

'Watch the woman.'

I wasn't happy with the task.

Jeanne d'Arlon turned her back to me. She adjusted her coiffure in front of the mirror. She powdered her face, already too pale, and reflexively refreshed her lips with a dab of lipstick.

At least twenty times in the last few hours, I had asked myself:

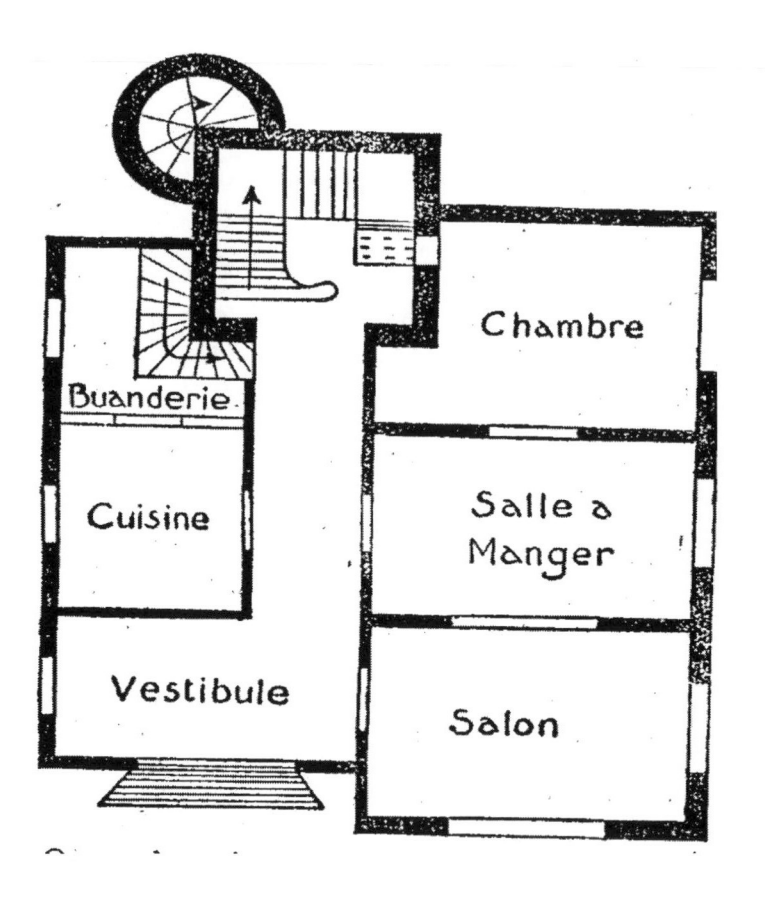

Buanderie = Laundry Room
Cuisine = Kitchen
Vestibule = Hallway
Chambre = Bedroom
Salle a Manger = Dining Room
Salon = Drawing Room

"Does she use lipstick?"

The answer was in front of me.

Her eyes met mine in the mirror. She looked away.

In the adjacent rooms, we could hear furniture being moved and shutters being closed.

Thanks to Troubert's organisational skills, the search of the ground floor was completed in ten minutes. The two groups reassembled, according to plan.

The inspector, satisfied, allowed himself a brief commentary:

'I've never seen a house as tightly sealed as this, if I may put it that way.

'Locks, bolts, shutters, everything is perfect. We are as secure here as if we were inside a safe.

'Due to the vigilance of the late Mme. de Nanteuil, no doubt.

'Now, my friends, we have a more agreeable task in front of us: to visit the cellar.

'Monsieur Dutheil! Position: the foot of the stairs. Mission: watch the stairs. No one must be able to come down from the first floor and slip into the ground floor rooms, certified as empty by Inspector Troubert.

'Madame d'Arlon, you will keep M. Dutheil company.'

'I would prefer—.'

'Ah, ah, ah. It's not a question of preference. I'm thinking of you, madam. You cannot be allowed to be alone in a house which is not yet secure.

'Here, Monsieur Dutheil, sit here.'

Troubert, full of solicitude, sat me down on one of the lower steps, with my back to the banister. He went to fetch a cushion from the drawing room, in order for Mme. d'Arlon to sit next to me.

'They look nice like that, the two of them, don't they?

'And if the chest thief comes downstairs, he'll have to climb over their heads.

'Are you coming, Monsieur d'Arlon?'

*****

'Please excuse me, madam,' I said, 'for this forced proximity.'

'It is I, sir, who should excuse myself for all the inconveniences I have caused you.'

I didn't dare respond with a gallant banality. It was not the appropriate time.

But I did find a subject of conversation by looking around.

'We are in an unusual position, but this staircase is even more unusual.'

'Don't talk like that. You forget you're supposed to know this manor since childhood.'

'True,' I said. 'And the circumstances are providential, in that they give you the opportunity to tell me what I don't know.'

To be honest, there was nothing odd about the staircase itself. It was the stairwell which was disconcerting. I had the impression of being at the bottom of a well, a square well, made of badly pointed blocks of stone. The coarseness of construction contrasted starkly with the rest of the building.

'I wouldn't want one of those blocks to fall on my head,' I said.

'They've been there for nine hundred years,' replied Mme. d'Arlon, 'and you have little to fear.

'This is the keep of the old Nanteuil Manor, an XIth century manor, of which only the relic is left. It was a refuge of pillaging Crusaders, one Thibault Tête de Laine amongst others.

'In the XVIIIth century, the Marquis de Nanteuil, my ancestor, demolished the remains of the old manor, except for the keep, which was too solidly built. And the new constructions lean against this keep.'

'Yes,' I said. 'I understand. The architect had an ingenious idea. He destroyed the horizontal partitioning of this tower and installed the main staircase here.

'But how did people go up or down the original keep?'

'They used a spiral staircase inside a turret, which still exists, and which you must have noticed when we drove round the manor.

'That staircase, in ruins, had become unusable and the accesses were walled up.'

'That patch of white plaster...?'

'Indicates where it came out. There was a door there once.'

'That's strange,' I said, looking around. 'I thought I heard something.'

'Oh!' said Mme. d'Arlon, 'that little walled-up staircase has its own inhabitants, you know.'

'What kind of inhabitants are you talking about?'

'Rats! The collapsed steps are still accessible to them. They're quite at home there. They come and go, just as Thibault Tête de Laine's men did.'

The noise did not reoccur.

I got up and went to bang my two fists against the walled-up orifice. I obtained the same hollow response everywhere.

'And what about that door?' I asked. 'Is that the old access to the keep?'

I pointed to a small arched doorway, symmetrical with the walled-up one.

'Yes. It would lead to my bedroom if it hadn't been sealed up as well, a long time ago, like the other.'

'What a collection of closed gates, walled-up staircases, and sealed doors,' I said, sitting down again. 'Anyone would think we were in an Anne Radcliffe novel.

'At least there are no ghosts, I assume?'

What an idiotic thing to say! The gaffe to end all gaffes!

That was all that was needed: evoking the corpse of Benoît Gérapin inside these old walls.

I didn't dare look at Jeanne d'Arlon any more.

'Why did you say that?' she murmured in a low voice.

I bit my lip so as not to respond.

'I know everything, you see… But I would rather die before telling anyone.'

I took a deep breath, which allowed me to detect a scent that was only too well known to me.

Was it the proximity of the young woman sitting less than a metre away from me? Or the too-precise evocation of the tragic cabin?

I reached to retrieve my cigarette case from the left pocket of my jacket. I wanted to chase away that scent for the second time. In so doing, I pushed down on the staircase step with my right hand. It brushed against Jeanne d'Arlon's, which she did not pull away….

It was barely a contact, but I could feel the warmth of the bare skin. I let the case fall back into the pocket. My heart was beating wildly.

Why wasn't she taking her hand away? Why was she encouraging this involuntary liberty? What did she want of me?

I sighed out of nervousness, and it seemed to me that the sigh was echoed. I moved my hand slightly, in order to affirm the light caress. Very gently, the bare hand was withdrawn....

My *sang-froid* only returned gradually. When I finally examined my neighbour out of the corner of my eye, I was surprised by her vacant expression.

What a remarkable actress this pale woman was.

She was staring straight in front at the corridor, as if I had ceased to exist, so help me!

Why did you just tolerate my touch, beautiful dreamer?

That was when my gaze alighted on her hand, and my heart, which had just recovered its normal cadence, stopped beating for a moment.

The hand was gloved.

CHAPTER III

The too-empty manor

I stood up so abruptly that Jeanne d'Arlon, frightened, stood up at the same time.

'What is it?'

Highly agitated, I looked all around us. And around us were a deserted corridor, a deserted staircase, and deserted rooms....

'What's the matter? Did you hear something? Say something....'

She approached me, to take my hands in her gloved ones. I recoiled nervously.

She stopped and considered me in silence.

'Hello, children,' came Troubert's voice from below. 'I have some good news to announce!'

Footsteps echoed on the stairs to the cellar.

Soon the door opened and Triel appeared.

'Have you found something?' asked Mme. d'Arlon.

'Judge for yourself.'

Troubert appeared in turn. His arms were full of dusty bottles.

'I have an announcement to make,' he said. 'Whatever else happens, we won't die of thirst tonight!'

He was followed by the chauffeur, Émile, similarly provisioned.

'Well, what is it, sentinels?'

My countenance, and Mme. d'Arlon's, must have given cause for suspicion.

Troubert immediately placed the bottles down on the tiles.

'Émile, my lad,' he said to the chauffeur, 'do as I do. That's called limiting the damage.

'What's happened to you, Monsieur Dutheil?'

'Just imagine,' I said, 'I believed....'

My explanation stopped there.

D'Arlon appeared in turn at the top of the staircase.

What could I say? How could I talk about the touching in which I'd been involved—the memory of which now gave me a shiver which

69

had nothing voluptuous about it.

'Monsieur Dutheil,' announced Jeanne d'Arlon, 'was impressed by the rats which fight each other in the holes of the old walls.'

There was a general outburst of laughter, lasting for a good thirty seconds.

After which, if I'm not mistaken, everyone became as worried as before—and maybe even more so.

'The incident is closed,' said Troubert, nevertheless, after having given us a long, hard look.

'The only thing left is for us to search the first floor. After which, I think we will have earned a refreshing meal.

'Are you coming with us, Monsieur Dutheil?'

'Why not?' I stammered.

*****

At the upper level of the keep was a Gothic window. I pressed my fevered brow against the hard, rusty bars. I avidly breathed in the cold night air, which had just hit me full in the face.

At that height, above the trees of Nanteuil, one discovered the rosy glow of Paris by night. The illuminated clock face of the Tour Eiffel showed only a few minutes past six. On the route to Saint-Germain, the beams of light from car headlamps crossed and uncrossed each other incessantly. The modern duel of light, seen through the bars of Thibault Tête de Laine, had something frightening about it.

The useless search finished without me. Since the team was looking in the dead-ended rooms on the first floor, dusty and three-quarters empty, there was no intercommunication for me to watch. And Troubert seemed more doubtful of my abilities now.

Behind me I could hear the few words exchanged between the searchers. I knew that, to my right, in one of the doorways, d'Arlon was speaking to his wife in a low, angry voice.

Troubert's voice approached suddenly, which caused me to shake.

'No need for thirty-six of us to go up to the eaves,' he was saying. 'It will be enough with me and Émile. Only there's no light up there.

'So, Émile, go down and find a few candles.'

'Very well, sir.'

'Dutheil? Where's Dutheil?

'I hope he hasn't been eaten by rats.'

'What is it?' I asked, turning round.

Troubert approached.

'My dear fellow, please have the goodness to return my revolver. I'm about to visit a dark old attic. If our presumed visitor is hiding there, which is not out of the question, I have no intention of being knocked out by him.'

'Excuse me,' I said, 'I should have returned it to you a long time ago.'

Except I couldn't find the revolver in question in any of my pockets.

'There, there,' said the inspector. 'Don't get upset, my boy, and don't bother looking in your jacket. I doubt that my Browning could take the place of your watch.'

He patted me down professionally.

'What's this? Have you dropped my revolver, now?'

The incident caused everyone to gather around us. For the second time that evening, I was the centre of attention.

I turned out all my pockets.

The revolver was certainly not on my person.

'Let's see, little one,' said Troubert, 'you do remember that I lent it to you, in order to allow you to watch the corridor?'

'Good Lord! I can clearly see myself, sitting on the red bench, with the weapon in my hand... And then later, on the step of the staircase....

'Ah! Sapristi!'

'What?'

'When I got up... Yes, at one point I got up to bang on the wall, behind which I'd heard suspicious noises... I slipped the revolver into my pocket... My right pocket, obviously.

'And that's where someone stole it afterwards, when I sat down again.'

'Who?'

'The bare hand!'

'What are you talking about?' asked Triel, whilst all the other spectators' eyes widened.

'What I mean is...' I stammered. 'I seemed to detect a slight rustling, just before you came out of the cellar. Now I think about it, maybe someone was in the process of taking the revolver out of my pocket!'

Troubert raised his arms to the sky. Triel, losing his habitual calm, grabbed me by the lapel of my jacket:

'You sensed that someone was searching you, and you didn't move?'

'No,' I said, my cheeks red and my temples sweating. 'At the time, I didn't attach any importance to it.'

Triel let go of my jacket.

'He's off his rocker,' said Troubert. 'But I'd still like to get my shooter back.

'Would you care to come down with me to reconstruct the scene, Monsieur Dutheil?'

We hadn't reached the ground floor, when he attacked me brusquely:

'So, she's the one who took the revolver, huh? Come on, admit it.'

'It wasn't Mme. d'Arlon,' I said.

'Hell's Bells,' swore the inspector, keeping his voice down so as not to be heard from the first floor, 'are you trying to make a fool out of me?'

'I repeat, Mme. d'Arlon didn't touch the revolver. I'm *absolutely* certain.'

'She was alone with you. She was sitting to your right.'

'She didn't do it.'

Something in my eyes or my voice must have shown my sincerity.

Mme. d'Arlon was coming down the stairs, followed by her husband.

'If only I could search her,' muttered Troubert. 'I'm sure I'd find something.

'But what can I do?'

'So,' asked d'Arlon, 'what's new?'

'We were happy to find the manor was empty,' growled the inspector. 'Now it's *too* empty.

'My revolver is missing.

'My only weapon, as luck would have it.'

'Strange,' said d'Arlon. 'Anyway, I hope the incident won't prevent you from having dinner?'

'I hope so, too,' said Troubert.

He muttered, turning his back to me:

'Except, as aperitif, I would have preferred something else.'

As far as I was concerned, it wasn't an aperitif I needed, but something much stronger.

CHAPTER IV

The dinner

Émile set the table, under the direction of Mme. d'Arlon.

The noise of the cutlery made a small, but irritating sound in the silence.

Then a dispute arose between d'Arlon, his wife, and Émile. There were six of us, including Émile, who were supposed to share the table. But seven settings had been laid.

Émile claimed he had taken the number of place settings prepared by his mistress. She claimed to have laid out the correct number.

D'Arlon imposed his authority and sent the extra setting back to the kitchen.

'Are you quite sure, dear friend, that you didn't invite anyone else to dinner? Or to partake of coffee?'

Mme. d'Arlon, her nerves on edge, broke a glass she was placing on the table.

'Breaking an empty glass brings good luck,' observed Troubert, quoting the old maxim.

*****

That was the incident which began our dinner at Nanteuil manor. Trivial enough in itself but, added to others, another stone in the edifice someone was constructing in the shadows....

A seventh guest, really?

Who amongst us would have been capable of receiving him?

D'Arlon, who was always preaching freedom, nevertheless took pains to lock all three doors of the room, connecting to the drawing room, bedroom, and corridor respectively.

Triel brought the chairs forward. Troubert uncorked the bottles.

We attacked the meal, which was composed mainly of cold meats and *charcuterie*—all that we had been able to find in the larder.

Mme. d'Arlon apologised:

75

'I've served you a really sad dinner, haven't I, gentlemen?'

That was also my opinion, but not just from the culinary point of view.

My gullet had shrunk to the point that I couldn't swallow a mouthful of ham without the accompaniment of a dangerous white wine, burning hot and ice-cold at the same time—from Jurançon, I believe—which Troubert replenished as necessary.

The conversation buzzed in my ears, without my paying much attention. Any allusion to the evening's events was strictly banned. I envied my companions, who were behaving more or less like normal people. It's true they didn't know of the existence of the bare hand.

In fact, what was the hand doing at that moment?

The dining room, which even lacked gaiety during the day, was positively sinister in the electric light. I found it suffered from the absence of a chandelier.

It was too vast for the lone lamp lighting it, under a lampshade from a general store. The corners were filled with shadow. The mirrors, with their corroded silvering, streaked with green threads like slices of Roquefort, sent back mouldy reflections.

'A slice of cold veal, Monsieur Dutheil? You're not eating.'

My eye remained fixed, not on the plate of veal, but on the hand which was offering it, a woman's hand, delicate and pale....

"It's bare, but it's too late," I said to myself. Did I think it out loud?

'What are you talking about, old man?' asked Triel anxiously.

'Nothing,' I said...'Er, thank you, madam, I'm really not hungry.'

'It's not going well with you, tonight,' said Troubert. 'A drop more Jurançon?'

I emptied my glass reflexively.

'What an awful meal I've provided for you,' lamented Mme. d'Arlon for the second time. 'I see that none of these cold dishes pleases M. Dutheil. Luckily, we have fresh eggs.

'Do you know how to make an omelette, Émile?'

'Assuredly, madam.'

'If you'll permit me, madam, I'll lend a hand,' said Troubert, instantly on his feet. 'I've been told the Chinese make their omelettes with hundred-year-old eggs, so I'm suspicious of their cuisine.'

Émile remained impassive.

'But...,' said Mme. d'Arlon.

'Whereas I,' continued Troubert, 'I know the veritable recipe of the omelette Saint-Michel. Allow me, you won't regret it!'

'If you insist.'

Troubert left the room and Émile followed him, carrying the dinner plates from the table.

'I believe above all,' said d'Arlon after the door was shut, 'that our friend Troubert doesn't want a yellow-skinned and little-known servant roaming free in the manor.'

'It's his duty,' said Triel.

'But don't get your hopes up about the omelette Saint-Michel.'

It was sound advice. The collaboration between the chauffeur and the inspector created, after a ten-minute wait, an omelette as black as the bottom of the pan underneath, and a prime candidate for most disastrous event of the evening.

'A little bit overdone,' admitted Troubert, who didn't seem the least embarrassed. 'But I'll make up for it with the coffee.'

And whilst Émile was serving the table, Troubert removed the cheese and the remains of the omelette.

*****

The comings and goings of the two of them, accompanied by the sound of locks being opened and closed, brought a certain relief to our anxieties. We had eaten badly but, thanks to Troubert, we had drunk well. The Jurançon had been followed by a rather decent Burgundy. A certain nervous gaiety, like that preceding the drawing of numbers at a lottery, pervaded the room. Mme.d'Arlon herself made an attempt to take part in the conversation.

I alone felt as though I had something stuck in my throat.

Troubert's coffee was excellent, but too strong. Drinking it increased my disquiet.

Had the coffee, by chance, been....

Everyone was drinking it, however.

Everyone except d'Arlon and the chauffeur, who had refused to drink any!

It seemed as though a new clairvoyance was awakening in me, aided by digestion. I forgot myself enough to stare at my host. A half-smile was flickering asymmetrically on his lips. His eyes were half closed behind the smoke from his cigarette. But there was a vigilant clarity in his regard.

Opposite him sat Jeanne d'Arlon, still just as pale, despite the small quantity of wine she had drunk. There was no doubt that she was sitting upright, she was talking, and she was smiling, but wasn't that just a supreme effort of willpower?

Were the badly-attached masks about to fall?

Wasn't the seventh guest already behind the door, brought by René d'Arlon from the other side of the world: vengeance?

What would happen in this dining room when we had rolled our chairs back and d'Arlon would be free to act?

The chauffeur was waiting, expecting orders. My God, it was he who had drugged the coffee!

And soon he would be one of the actors in the decisive scene, conceived under Asian skies, which the ancient French mirrors would reflect from every angle....

Horror!

My forehead beaded with sweat, I put my glass down on the table.

I shot a desperate glance at Triel. Triel had just emptied his cup of coffee.

Midnight sounded somewhere, the sound reaching us through who knows how many thicknesses of wall and floorboard.

At that moment, d'Arlon stood up.

The fog in front of my eyes dissipated.

But our host, slender and saturnine, said simply:

'I have the great pleasure of letting you taste a *marc* from Burgundy which is the crown jewel of the Nanteuil cellars.'

He filled the liqueur glasses.

He continued, without sitting down:

'And because a tragic chance brings us together at this hour of midnight, and also a sort of hostile will, let's drink to our encounter!'

Triel and Troubert were on their feet straight away, glass in hand, Troubert with a flushed face, Triel looking indifferent.

I stood up as well, forcing myself to appear convivial. Émile was on his feet, but without raising his glass, out of deference.

Mme. d'Arlon remained motionless.

'Well, Jeanne?'

The young woman stood up, her eyes holding her husband's gaze.

Her arm was extended and the liqueur glass trembled slightly. A drop of *marc* slid the length of the crystal.

'To all of the Nanteuil guests,' offered Troubert, 'visible and invisible!'

The last strokes of midnight faded away.

As I was bringing my glass to my lips, I heard three distinct, well-spaced knocks on the bedroom door.

08

CHAPTER V

The seventh guest

I choked on my *marc* and bent almost double, coughing and gasping. I had time to see Mme. d'Arlon let go of her glass, which broke on the table. Triel put his down without touching it.

'Who's there?' cried d'Arlon.

The timbre of his voice had changed.

No response.

'Enter!' shouted Troubert, who had downed his drink in a single gulp.

The door started to open.

I think I must have caught hold of the tablecloth, in order to keep my balance.

A thin sliver of black appeared between the door and the frame and grew slowly wider.

No creaking of hinges, no noise, not a breath!

Now the door was wide open. And nothing could be seen on the black screen stretched out in front of us. We were packed together, breathlessly, armed with table mats and dessert knives. I had picked up the coffee pot by its handle, a heavy, silver-plated coffee pot .

The bedroom didn't attack us, so we attacked the bedroom. Our group, bristling with miscellaneous weapons, advanced on the door like a fascinated animal.

We reached the threshold.

At that moment, the physical need to do something stretched our nerves to breaking-point. I remember the ornamentation on the coffee pot handle digging into the flesh of my fingers….

Ah! The furious fight, which abolished thought and fear!

Except that, on the other side of the dark threshold, there was only a void. The storm didn't break. Our arms were brandished against a Renaissance bed and an Empire writing desk….

The bedroom was empty, but it seemed to us that the seventh guest was now amongst us….

*****

I need to calm down. In order to write an intelligible account, I must forget my emotions at the time.

So, the room was empty. That was confirmed in less than five minutes.

We know the only two means of egress, apart from the connecting door we had come through, were: a shuttered window and a sealed arched doorway.

Now, the shutters had been latched shut *from the inside.*

And the bolts of the door had been shot *from the inside.*

No one, therefore, had been able to get out of the room.

I remember, as well, that d'Arlon had locked the drawing room door at the start of the dinner.

Who, then, had turned the key and pushed the door open?

'Whoever did this,' Troubert had said, in front of the wrought iron gate, 'whoever did this, stayed inside with us.'

Where was "whoever did this"?

An absurd association of ideas reminded me of a dessert plate from my childhood.

I killed two rabbits and a crow, where are they? And I turned the plate over, I turned it over….

Here, it was the décor which was turning before my eyes, like the revolving stage of the Théâtre Pigalle: the arched doorway, the drawing room door, the window, the old wall… Whilst d'Arlon moved the bed, Troubert opened the desk, each second that went by touched on the domain of the improbable and plunged us deeper and deeper into absurdity.

I collided with Triel, who seemed to be the only stable element in the assembled gathering… Triel, concerned but calm, with an attentive look….

'Who's there?' Troubert called out for the second time, abandoning the desk in order to go towards the drawing room we had just left.

I turned my head in his direction, just in time to see the aperture of the door go dark, at the same time a gentle click could be heard.

Someone had turned off the electricity in the drawing room.

Troubert stopped despite himself.

Then with a superhuman effort of willpower, he took a step

forward.

A cry escaped all our lips:

'Get back!'

Troubert stopped a second time, hesitant.

One could hear, coming from the darkened drawing room, a distinct creaking noise.

A tumult of terror caused us to spin around for a moment, like chickens with their heads cut off.

Then the door banged, slammed shut by Émile, and an irrational impulse propelled us towards it, to brace ourselves with the first furniture to hand, the enormous Empire writing desk, and to push it, pull it and drag it in front of the door.

In a few seconds it was done. We were barricaded in. Or definitely locked in—we didn't know which.

84

CHAPTER VI

The vigil

That we had been outmanoeuvred, lured there for who knows what purpose by a superior will to our own, was no more in dispute than the presence of a mediaeval wall at the far end of the bedroom.

No sooner had the writing desk been pushed against the door than an intense desire to flee seized us.

Yes, but where else to take refuge?

I placed my coffee-pot on the table, within easy reach.

Troubert wiped his brow with a chequered handkerchief. Émile awaited orders. We were good at giving orders!

D'Arlon wanted his wife to sit on the sofa. But she stood up and leant upright against the dividing wall.

The only sound now was our heavy breathing.

The awful, dire *décor!*

A red eiderdown slept between the twisted black columns of the Renaissance bed. The Empire desk blocking the door was as massive as a rock. Heavy two-handed swords hung crossed on the wall.

Mixed in with these enormous remnants of splendour, meteorites fallen from a bygone era, the wardrobe, the table and the sofa were shoddy bits of furniture which would have been crushed to pulp if the Empire desk had been in a bad mood.

Truth be told, there was no reason for the Empire desk to have been in a bad mood. But such an impression is characteristic of our state of mind at the time.

The same duality and opposition could be seen in the surroundings. The dividing walls were made of brick and plaster, and covered with vulgar wallpaper. But the walls of the keep, the famous XIth century walls, stood in contrast. Intruding almost one third of the way into the room, its rough stones were covered with mouldy tapestry and adorned with shiny trappings.

It was to this wall, in the final analysis, that we owed the impression of being irredeemably driven. It blocked the light. It muffled the sounds. It was as if, I repeat, someone was managing events, issuing silent orders through an invisible megaphone.

Someone murmured—I believe it was Troubert:

'Act like rats.'

Triel went over to the window. He checked the latches on the shutters, then opened them slightly in order to take a brief look at the park.

In fact, we weren't really prisoners, because we could still use that egress... Should we flee in the night, then, pursued by the invisible one?

Triel closed the shutters again. He went over to the writing desk to take a candlestick, which he placed in the middle of the table. His calm steps resonated in the silence.

'Have you a lighter, Monsieur Troubert?'

He lit the three candles. Without that precaution, which nobody had thought of, we would have run the risk of being plunged into total darkness at any moment.

For a moment, everyone looked at the three flickering flames.

Then each returned to his secret preoccupation.

D'Arlon and Émile stared at the door to the dining room as if they feared a new attack from that quarter, through a suddenly pulverised desk. Troubert paced up and down in front of the arched doorway like a dog who senses the enemy.

All the gestures and the rare words during those last moments remain engraved in my memory.

I saw the inspector's fingers grappling with the deadbolts locking the arched door, enormous square pieces of iron buried in monstrous housings. They were rusted and fused together. All Troubert's efforts to make them work were futile.

He let go, discouraged.

'To close things at Nanteuil is still possible. But to open them afterwards....'

He examined the lock.

'Is there a key?'

'I've never seen one,' replied Mme. d'Arlon.

Troubert left the door and went over to the wall, which he started to examine stone by stone and joint by joint.

A quarter of an hour went by in that fashion.

'Bah!' exclaimed Troubert, in a fit of exasperation, 'I've had enough with all these doors and windows. We're all going to go crazy before dawn! Do whatever you like, but do something!'

He made two or three rounds of the room, then, struck by a sudden idea, pulled a deck of cards out of his pocket, wrapped in a piece of old newspaper.

'Who knows how to play *belote*?'

'I do,' replied Triel.

'I played for two hours once, in a *bistro* in the rue Vavin,' said Troubert, in a grave voice, 'with someone who was only waiting for a moment's inattention to knock me out.

'I won every game.

'And I put him inside.'

'I'm sorry, but I don't know *belote*,' said d'Arlon.

Triel found common ground: *écarté*.

And I joined the three other players, so as not to admit my distress.

'After all,' said Troubert, drawing up his chair, 'we're not *chez* Fougeras here.

'We're not watching over a corpse, isn't that so?'

*****

A very unfortunate comparison. It was too much for Mme. d'Arlon's overwrought nerves.

We heard a sob, and the young woman's neck bent over.

'Well, Jeanne?' asked d'Arlon.

'There, there, madam,' said Troubert, trying to make amends. 'There, there, it was a misunderstanding.'

She cried, first in silence, then out loud, her face hidden in her hands, her shoulders shaking more and more. She was about to have a nervous breakdown.

D'Arlon went to her.

'Jeanne....'

'Leave me alone!' she cried out fiercely.

She looked up, her eyes wet with tears.

'Why are you all looking at me like that?' she exclaimed. 'What do you want from me? What do you think of me?

'What do you suspect me of? Say it! Say it!'

It was an admission which sprung to her lips, mixed with the moans, and Troubert, whose eyes were gleaming, didn't mistake it.

The creaking of a piece of furniture made her jump.

'I'm afraid,' she moaned.

'Who's there? Who's coming?'

She called out again to her husband:

'Don't come any nearer!'

Then, having noticed how he was looking at her, she went after Troubert:

'And you! You're trying to ambush me, aren't you? You're waiting for me to fall into your trap!

'You're all involved, all of you!'

An irresistible impulse brought me to the tortured young woman's side.

'Madam,' I said, in a voice full of emotion, 'we are two men here who have only known you for twenty-four hours.

'But I can assure you they will have to climb over our dead bodies to touch a hair of your head!'

CHAPTER VII

The shot

I thought I was being the gallant Chevalier de Lagardère (1).

But, in reality, I had created a diversion that was far from what I had intended.

The eyes of d'Arlon and Troubert were on me now.

'You've only known my wife for twenty-four hours?' exclaimed d'Arlon. 'Close confidant, eh! Childhood friend, eh!'

Mme.d'Arlon, who hadn't heard a word, sobbed even louder, her head buried in a cushion.

'Who are you? What are you doing here?' pursued d'Arlon, his face in mine.

How to reply?

I shoot a look of distress at Triel. But Triel is cold and is acting as if he's a stranger to the conversation.

And now d'Arlon turns on him.

'And you, the supposed Triel?'

'Excuse me?'

'I'm asking what you're doing here.'

'We're your guests,' replied Triel softly.

'Sir,' exclaimed d'Arlon, incensed, 'when one gives lessons in politeness to someone, one at least looks them in the face!'

It's true that Triel, wedged in his armchair in front of the table, no more moves his head than if he were suffering from a stiff neck.

'Sit down,' he says, indicating the armchair to his right.

D'Arlon, cowed by the other's calm, sits down without taking his eyes off him.

'Dutheil? Monsieur Troubert?'

In turn, we sit down at the table.

Triel starts to shuffle the deck of cards in front of him. Then he places it in front of d'Arlon.

(1) A gallant swashbuckling knight

'Cut, please.'

D'Arlon does as he is asked.

What is Triel doing? Is it working?

He deals out the cards, first three each, then two.

'Ah! What are you doing?' asks Troubert.

'I'm dealing the hands, as you can see.'

D'Arlon, who has reflexively picked up his five cards, throws them on the table.

'This tomfoolery has gone on long enough!' he says, white with anger. 'You are my guests, I acknowledge that. And you may assume that I'm very honoured. But I still have the right to ask you what you're doing here.'

Triel doesn't say a word.

'My questions are indiscreet, no doubt?'

'Not at all,' says Triel.

'Then what?'

'They're not indiscreet. But they're inopportune.'

'Really?'

'With your permission, I shall only reply tomorrow morning.'

Troubert gets his word in:

'Why is that?'

Triel replies, without turning his eyes towards the inspector:

'Because, tonight, there are more immediate preoccupations.'

'What are they?' exclaims d'Arlon.

'Wait,' replies Triel.

'You have a constant—and honourable—tendency, Monsieur d'Arlon, to forget the bizarre situation in which we find ourselves.'

He collects his cards, squares them up, and spreads them out in a fan.

'We're rather like the passengers on a small boat in deep waters,' he explains. 'Sudden movements and quarrels must be avoided. That's why I took the liberty of inviting you to sit in these armchairs.

'For, that way, I believe I can assure you we shall arrive safely in the harbour, that is to say, the dawn.

'Over to you, Monsieur Troubert.'

'What?' asks the inspector in surprise.

'It's your turn.'

Troubert picks out a card at random and, as luck would have it, it's the ace of trumps.

'Your turn, Monsieur d'Arlon!'

D'Arlon, bemused and intrigued, examines his cards.

It's touch and go as to whether we can even see the cards well enough to play this insane game. A fifty-candlepower lamp—an old carbon filament one, at a guess—is giving out a reddish-yellow glow.

The three candles in the chandelier add a dash of waxy yellow.

Together, that's the lighting of a 1905 motion picture film.

From the same period: the on-again, off-again game of the players, and the agonised face and dark-ringed eyes of Jeanne d'Arlon.

Add the shiny trappings on the walls, the twisted bed columns, and the silence, and you have the elements of pre-war cinema.

Émile is pacing up and down, throwing a gigantic shadow on the walls.

The cards fall on the table. The winnings are collected willy-nilly. Eyes look around the room more than they follow the game. It doesn't matter. The game is now in gear. Troubert wins.

'The queen of spades,' he announces. 'The sign of bereavement.'

'My turn to cut,' replies Triel.

He doesn't cut anything, because his card fades and becomes invisible as it reaches the table.

The electric light has just gone out.

A long and gradual extinction, proving that it is indeed an old carbon filament lamp.

*****

We're not in total darkness, because the three candles continue to burn. But the result is no less disastrous!

All the faces have changed.

Is it just because of the change of lighting?

Mme. d'Arlon has grabbed her husband's arm. For support? Or to immobilise him?

She is now illuminated as if by footlights. A new mask can be seen under the skin, a tragic one.

The floorboards crack under Émile's silent pacing.

With a gesture, Troubert bids him sit down.

Triel has pushed his armchair back so that his face is not in direct

91

candlelight.

'Well, the party goes on!' says d'Arlon, in a voice vibrant with the determination not to be outdone, but behind which cracks of fear can be detected.

And he cuts from the invisible deck a card which is even more invisible, for it's at that moment the room is plunged into *total* darkness.

Afterwards, everyone claimed to have seen the bundle of rags which crashed in our midst. But opinions varied as to the direction from which it had come.

For my part, I can vividly recollect the chandelier receiving a direct hit, and the candles describing incandescent arcs as they fall.

The third candle strikes the floor and goes out.

Pitch darkness. The clatter of overturned chairs. The frightful scream of Mme. d'Arlon and the call of her husband.

'Jeanne!'

And, dominating everything, the dry crack of the detonation.

For a fraction of a second, the bedroom lights up again. In the brief flash of the revolver, I see Triel on his feet with his arm half-extended in a shooting position, and the others caught in attitudes of astonishment.

And maybe a vague form facing Triel from the other end of the room.

Maybe....

For already the darkness has descended around us again.

CHAPTER VIII

The drop of blood

Nobody moved. Our thoughts seemed to form a disorganised jumble in the darkness.

Shadows danced in front of my eyes. It seemed as though blood was flowing in my temples like water in a pipe.

There followed a period of indeterminate length, because the only means of measurement, the steady beating of our hearts, had spun out of control.

Then three feeble lights followed one another in the darkness.

Troubert clicked his lighter and managed to get a flame on his fourth attempt. Our shadows appeared on the wall, flickering to the rhythm of the flame.

Setting suns, old light bulbs, candles and lighters... That our story was subject to a diminishing and more disparate light was one of its peculiarities. But it was true, nevertheless.

What was important was that there were six shadows. Six shadows on the walls!

And six flesh-and-bone people in the room. That was the normal nose count, do you understand? Which meant that, after the tumultuous hiatus, we all found ourselves in the same universe as before. We were all there! Mme. d'Arlon, with her deathly pallor and stricken countenance, was there. And no irregular shadow, no shadow detached from the body! I must have dreamt, when I thought I'd glimpsed for a moment....

'...a figure there, next to the door...'

Who had whispered that?

Whose was the finger that was pointing?

It was Troubert's.

Six pairs of eyes were now fixed on the wall of the keep, on which something had appeared for a fraction of a second....

Troubert went over to the arched doorway.

'What is it, then?' asked d'Arlon.

'What did you see?'

'Nothing much,' said Troubert, shaking the bolts of the arched door. 'Nothing much.'

But someone had been there, less than a minute ago!

*****

'But the bolts are still shot!' said d'Arlon, with a distinct nervousness.

Troubert, in the feeble light of his lighter, kicked the door hard several times, then ran over to the window to shake the bars.

Depending on where we were, some of us were in the light and some in the darkness at any given time. And each time a rapid gesture looked as if it might extinguish the flame, my heart leapt into my mouth.

'Everything's locked! Everything's locked!' shouted Troubert.

Triel collected the candles from the floor.

'Here, Troubert, come and light these.'

He had to grab the inspector's arm to calm him. He seemed to have gone mad.

Once the three candles were lit, some sense of security returned.

'Someone was there, less than a minute ago!'

'Never!' exclaimed d'Arlon. 'How could he have got in?'

'And this,' I said, 'how could this have got in?'

I brandished the bundle of rags which had extinguished the chandelier.

Troubert took it, felt it, sniffed it in vain and stuck it under d'Arlon's nose.

'And this, how could this have got in?'

'I didn't see anything,' insisted d'Arlon.

'And you, Triel?'

'I don't remember anything in particular,' replied Triel.

I thought the inspector's eyes would pop out of his head.

'You didn't see anything. You didn't see anything,' he said, in a low voice.

'Yet it's you who fired the shot!'

'Yes.'

'At whom?' shouted Troubert.

'At no one.

'I fired at random, to reassure everyone.'

Troubert leant against the old wall, touched it, then pivoted to face Triel.

'You fired a revolver to reassure everyone... Where's the bullet?'

'I lost my head,' said Triel.

Troubert opened his mouth but no sound came out. He needed to catch his breath.

'I thought you hadn't got a revolver,' he said eventually.

'Why?' said Triel. 'You never asked me.'

He opened his hand, in which a metal object gleamed.

Troubert turned to look at Mme. d'Arlon, seated on the arm of one of the armchairs. But her attitude was such that he dared not ask her, not now, not ever, whether she had seen a vague figure at the end of the room.

The inspector pushed against the rear wall.

'Ah!' he said, with an extraordinary expression, which was a mixture of anger and fear, 'I would much prefer that revolver were in my hands, rather than anyone else's.'

'It's all yours,' said Triel.

He put the weapon down on the table.

Nobody touched it.

Troubert stared at us distractedly.

Pale face of Jeanne d'Arlon, tense face of her husband, impassive face of chauffeur... Inscrutable face of Triel... Obtuse face of old arched doorway ....

Truly, we were surrounded by faces of mystery. And, superimposed, was the face of Gérapin and his sneer.

Troubert dropped into an armchair.

He had been affected, and was taking it hard.

That was when his eye, wandering mechanically over the floorboards, made the last memorable discovery of the night: a drop of blood.

A fresh drop, bright red.

It was on a line going directly from Triel's armchair to the arched doorway. Triel had fired into the void, *but the void had bled.*

CHAPTER IX

The traveller

That spring morning, blue with threads of gold, was as pretty as a dessert plate. I was sitting on a pile of dead wood. I let the breeze caress my newly-shaven cheeks.

Alas! It would have required a tornado or a cyclone to sweep away the clouds which burdened my spirit.

I tried to concentrate on the interplay of the sun and the branches.

But the film which kept playing in my mind was that of the closed gate, the drive in the car, the toast drunk in *marc du Bourgogne*. It was the game of *écarté*, the flash of the revolver shot, the appearance of the vague figure....

And, afterwards, everything becoming blurred around a drop of implacably shiny blood.

Heavy knocks echoed in my daydreaming. In a fit of exasperation, we broke down the arched doorway, using the bench from the hallway. We pulled away the stones walling off the concealed staircase. But behind the plaster and the broken panels there was only dust disturbed in vain, only a void....

*****

No less empty were the hours of torpor which followed.

Jeanne d'Arlon, stretched out on the bed, was sleeping, or pretending to... Her husband, standing next to her, incompetent doctor or clumsy executioner, one didn't know which... The rest of us, scattered in various chairs and armchairs with aching heads, staring at now-open doors, through which no further attack came.

Slowly, very slowly, the light of dawn yellowed the glow of the candles.

*****

A dry cracking sound, and I give a violent start.

Who's there?

But no, I'm still in the Nanteuil park, in the open air and full sunlight.

What's approaching is not a ghost but a woman.

And what woman other than Jeanne d'Arlon would be haunting this lost trail?

She's wrapped in the grey coat she was wearing yesterday evening, next to Gérapin's corpse. Her hat is of the same neutral colour and makes her appear to fade in the morning mist. But a small blue overnight case she's holding in her right hand keeps her in the real world.

The sun's in her eyes and she hasn't yet noticed me. Can't she sense the burning look in my eyes?

I get up so clumsily that I stub my toe on a log and almost fall flat on my face.

When I regain my balance, I see her facing me, motionless, ten feet away.

And all I can find to say is:

'Are you taking the air, madam?'

She doesn't reply.

I adjust my tie.

'After such a night, one needs to clear one's head, doesn't one?'

'Were you lying in wait for me?' she asks, paying no attention to my words.

'Me? How could you believe such a thing?'

My face must have shown my innocence.

She notices, but doesn't smile.

'All right.'

After a moment's hesitation, she continues, her eyes lowered:

'Well then, I don't regret the meeting.'

'Really?' I say, elated.

'Yes. I know I owe you an apology. I beg your pardon.'

'Pardon for what, madam?'

'This sinister adventure in which I involved you, you and your friend, and which was so strange to you.'

I protest, but she continues to ignore what I say.

'It has all been so pointless….'

I remember her comment from the previous evening :

'Tragedy entered here before you did.'

Ah! Isn't the diligent visitor to Nanteuil wearing a grey travel coat and carrying a blue overnight case?

'It's all over now.'

'What's all over, madam?'

She makes a gesture like someone waving smoke away.

'I'm leaving.'

'Permit me to point out that the path you're on leads nowhere.'

'On the contrary, perhaps it leads very far away.'

A warbler starts to sing, perched on the end of a branch three paces away from us.

'It's true,' I said, 'that at least one person has taken this path, for a very long voyage....'

She understands that I'm referring to Benoît Gérapin and her expression hardens. So it is that, up to the last, the memory of the hanged man hovers over us.

She grasps the handle of the overnight case.

'You do know,' I say, 'that I shall not let you pass.'

'Really?'

'Really. I will not, I cannot let you leave on who-knows-what adventure.'

I add, in cowardly fashion:

'Or else let me come with you.'

'No.'

The tone is very firm.

The warbler gets its breath back and embarks on another suite of variations.

'Then you shall stay!'

I secretly hope for an outburst of anger, a revealing spark in those beautiful eyes.

But no, only a bitter smile.

'Men are strange,' she says, 'even the best of them. I don't think, Monsieur Dutheil, that you will allow yourself to retain me against my will, even though the circumstances make it possible.

'At this moment, you are playing with my very existence.'

'Madam, it was you who called us here to defend you.'

'And you think that, by holding me here, you're defending me?

'The adventure… You say you fear me leaving on who knows what adventure.

'Do you know what the worst possible adventure would be, the most inexorable?'

I fear I know the answer, but the response follows the question.

'It would be to remain here.'

I say nothing, but she senses her words have struck home.

'I *must* leave!'

Then, in a whisper:

'It was I who killed him.'

I bite my lip to avoid crying out:

'I knew!'

She takes a step forward, so she is very close to me. Her eyes are shining, as they were in the cabin where the murder took place.

'So? Do you want to lose me?'

'How ironic,' I say. 'I'm going to lose you anyway.

'If only you would accord me….'

'What?'

I don't pursue the matter.

I've remembered all too suddenly the red mark on the lips of the other, the indefinable scent on his clothes… No, not that….

I step back despite myself.

You're free to go, traveller.

'One last word, madam,' I say, as she goes past. 'When I think of you—and I fear it will be often—what should I think?'

She turns her head away, so I shall never know the expression she wears, and pronounces these last words:

'Never think of me again. I am dead to you and to the rest of the world.'

She leaves, frightening the warbler, who flies away….

CHAPTER X

Searches

In the early afternoon, the Nanteuil estate started to swarm (Troubert vocabulary) in a strange fashion. On the pathways, the first mourning clothes could be seen, worn by the Gérapin and Fougeras families, notified by telegramme. At the same time, the plain-clothes suits of the police could be seen, coming in support of Troubert.

The former set up their headquarters in the concierge's lodge, and the latter in the manor. Each regarded the other with suspicion, should they happen to meet.

The event held an unexpected importance, due to the disappearance of Mme. d'Arlon.

At two o'clock, following a series of confrontations, a dozen people gathered in the manor, under the auspices of a special commissioner whose name I forget.

Encountered in the corridors: Troubert, who had just finished lunch, purple in the face, happy, and half-drunk; d'Arlon, pale and badly shaved, who had spent the mealtime alone in his room.

I had the honour of starting the meeting. I had to provide a detailed account of my encounter with Mme. d'Arlon in the park.

The commissioner looked at me through enormous spectacles which concealed the expression in his eyes. He looked just like one of my family's doctors, to whom I'd had to confess some youthful errors. Which only served to increase my unease.

'So,' he said, 'do you find it natural to meet young women in travelling clothes, at nine o'clock in the morning, in lost paths in this park?'

'Mme. d'Arlon was on her own property,' I said. 'I couldn't bring her back to the manor by force.'

'You could at least have alerted Inspector Troubert, sir, about what you'd just seen. That would have allowed him to take the initiative, even if you felt you could not.'

'That's what I did.'

'That's what you did after a delay of an hour and forty minutes! You wouldn't have acted otherwise if you'd been complicit with the fugitive.'

'Excuse me. It would have been easier still for me to have said nothing.

'I'm not an informant, after all. If your police are incapable of surveilling people they suspect, it's not my job to fill in for them.'

After ten minutes of similarly unfriendly dialogue, the commissioner, wiping his spectacles the better to stare at me, asked:

'Would you be so good as to tell us why you've been here for the last twenty-four hours?'

I hesitated. Triel interceded on my behalf:

'We were called here by Mme. d'Arlon.'

'It's not you I'm questioning, sir!' exclaimed the commissioner.

I confirmed what Triel had said. I handed over, as evidence, the lilac letter, which had never left my pocket.

'Very well,' said the commissioner, without further question, but keeping the letter.

Then, going back to the disappearance of Mme. d'Arlon, he called for the Fougeras family, in order to determine as accurately as possible the time of the disappearance.

The wife provided vital testimony. She had seen Mme. d'Arlon walk through the gate approximately five minutes after having met me. Mme. d'Arlon had nodded slightly to indicate: *au revoir*. She hadn't spoken to her.

'She passed by like a shadow, like someone no longer of this world. It had quite an effect on me!'

Old Fougeras merely confirmed his wife's account.

And so the trail that I had contributed to reconstructing led to the Nanteuil estate gate. The magic gate! Beyond it, nothing.

No one, either in Marly, or in Bougival, had seen the fugitive. No suspicious car had been seen. Two or three sightings had been reported, but they had turned out to be wrong.

'Well, gentlemen,' said the commissioner, raising his spectacles, 'I thank you. Next!'

We left the drawing room.

D'Arlon, who was wandering around like a lost soul, came to find out what point the investigation had reached. Soon after, he edged away, excusing himself, and went back to his room. He claimed to be dead from fatigue.

I remained with Triel in the corridor with the black and white tiles. We weren't quite sure what to do. We sat on the bench with the red velvet cover, opposite the umbrella stand, which was now crowded with half-a-dozen walking sticks and umbrellas.

Hardly had we sat down when Triel, struck with an idea, made me stand up so he could lift the lid.

It was empty—just like the night before.

'What,' I said, 'have you reached that point?'

'Yes, I have. And so have the others in the drawing room.'

The doors of the drawing room opened shortly thereafter.

Troubert emerged, twirling his disgusting boater round his finger.

He winked in our direction and came over.

'Good day, colleagues,' he said.

'Good day, colleague,' replied Triel.

'You know, from the moment I set eyes upon you, I said to myself: those are colleagues. Amateur colleagues.

'When you have the eye....'

'Your eye didn't let you down.'

'So, I believe we're at the same point, amateurs and professionals?'

'Unfortunately.'

'The others can take their turn,' continued Troubert jubilantly. 'They're all going to come round. They'll crawl on all fours, sniff the dust in the old carpets.

'They won't find anything. They'll begin to believe that we, the rest of us, dreamt what happened last night.

'Between the three of us, they wouldn't be altogether wrong. There must have been something like that.'

'Really?'

'Yes, we've been a bit too impressionable. The hanged man, the little game with the doors—and the Jurançon, and that damned coffee, which was much too strong—all that got on our nerves.'

I couldn't help asking:

'And the bundle of rags? And the drop of blood?'

Troubert fanned himself with his boater, like a lady with her fan.

'Listen,' he said, 'take the advice of an old professional.

'Two things are certain in this whole business:

'Benoît Gérapin hanged himself.

'Mme. d'Arlon ran away.

'That's *terra firma*. That's a base of operations!

'Start by locking up the woman. I'm telling you right now, she'll talk. And a lot of details will be explained: drop of blood, bundle of rags and more….

'I'm leaving you, gentlemen.'

'You're going out?'

'Yes.

'There's a lot of business for me outside. The tramline, the taxis, the stations….

'I'm not a man who works indoors. The trips between the gate and the front door, between the bedroom and the drawing room, that's not my kind of work. Now, I'm going to get busy.

'I'm a big boy and I'm generous. I give Mme. d'Arlon forty-eight hours. In forty-eight hours, maximum, she'll be back in the fold, with two strong guard dogs.

'And you? What are you going to do?'

'We're staying,' replied Triel. 'I'm going to keep looking, inside Nanteuil itself.'

'That's a valid option. The idea's a bit bizarre, but it's an option.

'Wait a minute. Do you want someone to help?

'Frankly, we have too many officers here. Mouron! Hey, Mouron!'

'I can assure you,' said Triel, 'it's useless.'

'Let me be the judge. Only too happy to be of service.

'Mouron! Are you deaf?'

The individual who had been hailed, who had been pacing up and down in front of the manor entrance, approached with bad grace.

In fact, it wasn't Mouron. It was a member of the Fougeras family, who had been walking around, clad in a black coat and wearing a bowler hat.

'Excuse me,' said Troubert, 'I mistook you for someone else.

'What are you doing there, anyway? Did anyone send for you? No. So?'

Troubert turned towards me:

'Talk about an environment for conducting an investigation. There's an unknown face at the corner of every path.'

He shot a bitter glance at the retreating man.

'They can't bury Gérapin quickly enough.'

'It's tomorrow, I believe?'

'Tomorrow morning.

'Tomorrow morning,' repeated the inspector thoughtfully.

'I'll try to be there, if the lady of the manor hasn't already been found.

'It's always interesting, a burial. You see people...You have a drink when it's over. You listen to people....

'Will you be there?'

'Not on your life,' I said.

'Of course we'll be there!' exclaimed Triel, whose voice was louder than mine. 'We wouldn't miss it for anything, knowing those poor people.'

'Here's Mouron anyway,' said Troubert. 'I hope it's the real one this time. I'll order him to be at your disposal.

'Good luck, gentlemen. It's been a pleasure, in a manner of speaking.'

'The pleasure was all ours.'

CHAPTER XI

The faded paper

'He's a happy man,' I said to Triel, when the inspector was out of earshot.

'He's relieved more than anything,' replied Triel. 'Mme. d'Arlon, by fleeing, assumed complete responsibility for the whole business. They'll charge her with all the sins of Nanteuil.

'A culprit! What more could the inspector ask for?'

'What a curious inversion of roles,' I said.

'Inversion?'

'Up until now, Triel, you've been thought of as superior, even disdainful. It was touch and go whether Gérapin's corpse or the phantom of the bedchamber would drag a gesture or a smile out of you. "This riddle is a little too simple for me," you seemed to imply.'

'And then?'

'Then the riddle gets more complicated. Your brows knit vertically and the corner of your mouth turns down bitterly. You're out of ideas.'

'Imbecile!'exclaims Triel furiously. 'Happy imbecile. You're the one who got us into this mess.

'By some miracle, you run into that woman at nine o'clock in the morning, on the obscure pathway she's using to flee the premises. You bare your soul to her—and you let her leave.

'The commissioner was right, just now. You have about as much initiative as a sign post.'

'You understand nothing of chivalrous feelings.'

'I only understand one thing: if Jeanne d'Arlon is no longer alive at this hour, the responsibility is on your head!'

The afternoon hours dragged on interminably.

Triel searched every bush in the park in vain. The Mouron fellow, charged by Troubert to help us—and keep an eye on us—never let him out of his sight.

As for me, after Triel's tirade I was incapable of intelligent work. All I could do was wander around the most remote corners of the park, under the flowering trees.

Sometime that evening, the special commissioner left Nanteuil, no doubt judging that his investigation was concluded. Just as Troubert had predicted, all the efforts were concentrated on finding Mme. d'Arlon.

How many more times would that woman, left to her own devices, evade the police net?

'Not for much longer,' Mouron, the authorized recipient of Troubert's thoughts, assured us.

Nevertheless, as night fell, no news from the outside had reached us. Troubert and Triel shared a common lack of success.

Everyone abandoned the manor.

D'Arlon took a room in the hotel *Cheval d'Or* and dined in his room.

Triel and I ate in a small restaurant in the same hotel, in the company of Mouron and one of his colleagues, by the name of Ventadour.

The two men had taken a liking to us that was as sympathetic as it was sudden.

They showered us with Burgundy wine.

Perhaps they had their own ideas about the goings-on at Nanteuil. Perhaps they were looking for an original solution along the lines of Triel-Dutheil. If that were the case, they certainly paid for the privilege.

But if all they wanted to do was to get us to talk, they succeeded admirably. What did we have to hide?

I gave a complete account of the events of the previous night, and I did it a couple of times. Triel watched me placidly, only intervening to make elliptical remarks.

Only once did he comment directly, but it was so bizarre that I didn't know what to think.

I was in the midst of deploring the mediocre part I had played in the affair, as a journalist.

'Who would have thought,' I said, 'that the death of Benoît Gérapin would be but the prelude to such an obscure tragedy. Alas! I was on the spot, but I didn't take any initiative. On the contrary, because of an excessive discretion regarding my hosts, I scribbled a few banal lines about the basic facts; a paper which completely faded away from one day to the next.'

The expression caught Triel's attention.

'That's very colourful,' he said. 'Faded paper! The concierge said that about the beautiful wallpaper in her bedroom with the flower pattern that the sacrilegious sun had bleached prematurely. It is thus that the vocabulary of journalism is enriched.

'Never mind. It's expressive. One can immediately see friend Dutheil's telegramme yellow and shrivelled.'

The two policemen looked indulgently at Triel. The vapours of the Burgundy, they told themselves....

As for me, I had asked myself the precise meaning of the remark, but had not been lucky enough to put my finger on it.

Triel had fallen silent again, thinking about something else—or giving the matter deeper thought.

I slept badly that night. The shadow of Jeanne d'Arlon disturbed my dreams, in which expresses rumbled noisily past and the Seine flowed silently. I was obsessed by Triel's words.

"If Jeanne d'Arlon is no longer alive at this hour..."

It was already broad daylight when Triel woke me up.

'All right, let's get up!'

'What's up?' I asked, my mind still full of sinister images.

'Get up! We're going to Benoît Gérapin's funeral.'

CHAPTER XII

Benoît Gérapin's funeral

Ding... Dong....

The church clock let its sonorous notes fall on us like drops of rain.

The wind was fresh and the sky overcast. The funeral procession followed an interminable, hilly path bordered by high walls, behind which rose barren treetops.

I walked behind the family, to the left of d'Arlon. To the left of d'Arlon's earthly presence, I should say. For his spirit, I can say with some confidence, was following another funeral along unknown paths. There had been no news of Jeanne d'Arlon during the day. Searches in Nanteuil had turned up no clues. Now it was the turn of the hospitals and the morgues.

'Talk about a climb,' said a familiar voice suddenly. 'The dead must think they're being taken directly to heaven.'

It was Troubert, coming to join us, eternal boater in hand. He kept step badly and spoke too loudly. I was moderately glad to see him again.

He was already asking questions.

'Why is the clock chiming? There's no religious service, is there?'

'It's not tolling for Gérapin,' I said. 'There's another ceremony.'

'Where's Triel? Isn't he with you?'

'He's in the procession somewhere. We lost sight of each other as we left the mortuary.

'He may be at the rear.'

'I didn't see him, even though I looked. Any news?'

'None.

'And you?'

'None!

'The amateur and the professional are equal. They both have nothing.

'At least until a new order.'

Mechanically, Troubert placed his boater on his head and removed it immediately.

'I don't know about you,' he said, 'but I don't like burials without a service. I find it sad.'

The sound of the bells receded little by little.

The path flattened out and there was a break in the high walls. We found ourselves on a plateau used for cultivating market garden produce. The wind smelled of humus.

'It'll rain within the half-hour,' predicted Troubert. 'Is it far, their damned cemetery?'

'It must be that little wall, over by the clump of trees.'

'Let's hope so. Talk about a long slog.

'Do you know that we police walk more kilometres than postmen?'

I didn't bother to reply.

Troubert continued nevertheless:

'Something I find fascinating. Have you noticed that funeral processions stretch out over several hundred metres? There are some stragglers for whom even that pace is too fast. They can't keep up!'

We finally arrived at the cemetery gate. There was a regrouping, during which I lost sight of Troubert.

To be frank, I was partly responsible. To make up for it, I ran into Triel.

'There you are!' I said. 'Where have you been?'

'I got lost,' he said breathlessly, like someone who's just finished a race. 'I wandered away from the procession somehow, and had to rush to catch up.'

There were drops of perspiration on his forehead, despite the fresh air.

He mopped them with his handkerchief.

'Really?' I said. 'I think you're pulling my leg.'

Triel looked at me for the first time, and it was a luminous, dilated look, like the eye of a cat in the darkness.

And it wasn't destined for me. Triel looked right through me as he pursued his reverie somewhere beyond.

'Everyone's here, I hope?' he asked in a low voice.

He stood on tiptoe to get a better view of the attendees.

'Goodness me,' I said, 'what have you been doing for the last half-hour? Your hands are black with dust, for heaven's sake!'

Triel frowned.

'Shove off!' he replied.

I turned purple with anger and surprise.

Luckily, our conversation was in whispers. Nobody heard us, I hoped.

The march started again, to the sound of dragging soles. The narrow path we were on obliged everyone to walk closer together. I had to march shoulder-to-shoulder with Triel.

People stopped and arranged themselves, more or less, around a rectangular hole. The jostling of the crowd caused me to step in a pile of loose earth, from which I had trouble extricating myself.

The ceremony wound down. Opposite us, several women sobbed beneath their black veils. Triel's radiant gaze took it all in.

I felt his hand, as hard as a pair of pliers, grip my left forearm.

Triel whispered in my ear:

'How do you like the funeral?'

I felt like saying:

'Shove off!'

But I merely shrugged my shoulders to indicate the question was not worthy of a response.

'I find it marvellous,' said Triel, half closing his eyes.

'It's the most beautiful funeral I've ever attended.'

The coffin, badly suspended, descended askew. The women's sobs intensified.

'Look at d'Arlon's face,' whispered Triel.

The unfortunate man certainly made a sad figure as he watched his entire existence descend into the muddy hole.

'Hilarious, isn't it?'

'Keep your voice down,' I hissed.

I was beginning to wonder if Triel had been drinking. Whether he hadn't sneaked away to get drunk.

Eventually the ceremony ended, to the sound of shovelfuls of earth being flung on the coffin. The circle of attendees opened, a black garland whose knot had come undone. A fine rain accentuated the impression of disarray. The ground, scraped twice by thick soles, was already turning into mud.

At the cemetery gate, a vestige of decency slowed down those trying to get away. Lined up against the gate were three black figures:

the family, in the order Old Fougeras, his wife and their daughter.

Everyone stood aside to allow d'Arlon to leave first. D'Arlon himself ceded to us, purely out of politeness.

'I'm not going to do that,' said Triel who, in an excess of deference, stepped back onto my feet.

So it was that d'Arlon went first, followed by Triel, then me, then Troubert. Mutterings of vague condolences, gripping of cotton gloves.

It was over. We were outside.

The rain became heavier.

Troubert, who hadn't bothered to bring a coat, for whatever reason, turned up his jacket collar. Drops of water shone like miniscule stalactites around the perimeter of his boater.

'Let's stay awhile, if you don't mind,' he said. 'The train to Paris leaves in half an hour. And since I no longer have any reason to stay in this hamlet....'

'You're abandoning the case?'

'I'm not the one responsible for finding Mme—.'

He stopped, shooting a look at d'Arlon, whose silent presence he had forgotten.

But d'Arlon wanted to appear off-hand.

'I believe the matter is over for everyone. For my part, I intend to return to Saigon on the boat leaving on the twenty-fifth.'

No one said a word.

'Obviously, if there is any new information, I would be obliged if you would notify me.'

'You may count on it,' replied Triel.

We raced down the hill we had climbed up so laboriously behind the hearse. Rivulets of water were now running in every direction.

The farewells we exchanged at the entrance to Marly were brief and restrained. They made no mention of the memorable hours we had spent together.

'I shall be going to Paris as well,' said d'Arlon. 'My car is stationed a stone's throw from here. Would you care to join me?'

'Willingly,' said Troubert.

I opened my mouth to say as much. Triel silenced me with a sharp jab in the ribs.

'Excuse us,' he said, 'but there's a matter we have to take care of here.'

Troubert and D'Arlon looked up in surprise. The inspector's eyes were almost phosphorescent.

'A matter you have to settle?'

'Yes,' said Triel. 'Our hotel bill!'

Everyone burst out laughing.

Two minutes later, d'Arlon's car started up.

The old and pathetic 10CV, which had carried us around the estate in pitch darkness, into dead-end alleyways. I was filled with emotion to see it leave.

I was alone with Triel.

The rain became even heavier.

THIRD PART

CHAPTER I

Above Nanteuil

'Yes, sir… Very well, sir… I'll tell the gentleman.'

The receptionist hung up the telephone with a slight click reminiscent of a revolver being cocked.

He turned towards me.

'M. d'Arlon asks that you go up, sir.

'It's on the second floor, on the corridor to your right, room twenty-three.

'The lift is at the foot of the stairs.'

But I preferred to walk up, to give me time for one last reflection.

I stepped into the hustle and bustle of the hotel.

Doors opened onto rooms where beds were being made. Brooms banged against plinths. A maid hummed an air from *Tosca*. A light dust floated in the cage of the staircase.

I stepped on a breakfast tray and broke the handle of a cup.

'Come in!'

D'Arlon had just finished shaving. He was rubbing his cheeks with an alum stone, which, held between two fingers and pierced by a ray of sunlight, sparkled like a diamond.

'Pray excuse me. I've finished, by the way.'

'Please.'

I took a chair whilst d'Arlon was finishing his beauty care. I repeated to myself once again the sentences I was about to utter.

"Monsieur d'Arlon, when you left us eleven days ago…"

Powder, now?

The supposed widower was certainly conscious of his appearance.

And a little affected, into the bargain.

"Monsieur d'Arlon, when you left us eleven days ago…"

All around us, the noise of Marseille filled the space. We couldn't see the sea, but it was omnipresent, from the wailing of the sirens to the vague odours it sent towards the town….

Finally, d'Arlon turned towards me.

'To what do I owe the pleasure?'

'Monsieur d'Arlon,' I said in a rush, 'when you left us eleven days ago, on a street in Marly, you said the following: "if there is any new information, I would be obliged if you would notify me."'

'And what is this new information?'

'Mme. d'Arlon has been found.'

'Alive?'

'Yes.'

D'Arlon didn't bat an eyelid.

For two whole minutes he stood facing his mirror, with his back towards me.

I suddenly suspected that, during this time, he was forcing himself to compose a mask of impassivity.

How should I get through to him now?

It was he who seized the initiative.

He pulled up a chair and sat down facing me.

'Speak, sir. I'm listening.'

I was prepared to handle many things, but not this glacial welcome which was like a bucket of cold water. I forgot my carefully prepared phrases.

'Well?' said d'Arlon.

'Your wife has been found,' I said stupidly. 'However, is she really your wife?'

D'Arlon's eyes widened.

'What I mean to say is,' I continued, mumbling in my desire to break the news gently, 'do you really know who your wife is?'

Faced with the other's attitude, I hastened to add:

'I don't want to keep you in suspense, but please let me explain in a logical fashion, otherwise you won't understand anything.'

'Where's my wife?'

'I don't know myself.'

'Did you come here to make a fool of me?' said d'Arlon, in a voice which must already be audible outside the room.

'I can get up and leave,' I said.

'Stay,' said d'Arlon, with a murderous look. 'But, for God's sake, stop approaching the subject in a crabwise manner!'

'I repeat that I have to explain....'

'Then explain, for the love of God. I've been waiting for five minutes.'

I made a great intellectual effort.

'You're familiar with the Nanteuil estate.'

'It would seem so!'

'Well then, Monsieur d'Arlon, everything is in the configuration, the topography of that estate.

'Yes,' I continued volubly, for I had remembered the line of reasoning I had prepared, 'everything is there. Please bear with me for a moment. Lift yourself up and imagine yourself above Nanteuil, so you can see the whole estate at once. Now go back ten years, to the genesis of the current drama.

'What do you see, at the centre of all the swathes of green? The manor. The manor, the central cell, but withered and dying. An old woman and a child vegetating inside those old walls....

'To one side, the living cell, the concierge's lodge. Old Fougeras, his wife, their daughter Élise, their nephew Benoît; they prune, weed, plant, cultivate and harvest.

'For the benefit of the two hermits in the manor, no doubt, the two fallen queens? Let's see...

'Let's see, because the current matter is possibly the outcome of an antagonism carved into the very ground... The absorption of the old cell by the new... A peasant revolt several metres square!

'In short, the attack on the manor by the Fougeras family.'

D'Arlon, who had been listening without suspecting what I was leading up to, and without the slightest sign of comprehension, suddenly seemed to perceive a spark in the night, and reacted by repeating mechanically:

'The attack on the manor by the Fougeras family?'

'Why not? An attack which follows a predetermined curve, which you cannot fully detect, even now.'

CHAPTER II

The sealed door

'Now, on that silent battlefield, fate brings three visitors together simultaneously: Triel, myself—and Death.

'And, when I say fate… you will soon see that fate has a face.

'Nobody answers the door bell. We push the door open and go in.

'The Fougeras residence is deserted. Potatoes are boiling in the pot. The setting sun is yellowing the wallpaper….

'There's a click—not even that, more a wink—and the peaceful décor has been photographed. And not because I'm in the habit of carrying a Kodak around with me. That would be pointless; Triel possesses an apparatus just as effective—his eye.

'The Fougeras' bedroom is filed in the cerebral archives that evening, in full colour. Including the nuances in the wallpaper. Don't tell me I'm getting lost in useless detail: the whole mystery of Nanteuil lies in those nuances.

'Panorama of the park. Then the lens alights on a macabre subject: Benoît Gérapin's corpse. Close-up.

'You, Monsieur d'Arlon, run towards the manor in search of a knife. Triel rummages, sniffs, examines puddles of water and stares at the hanged man with the greatest of interest. He seems to be working in a vacuum. In reality, he has discovered a number of small things, including this: the dead man's lips are just a bit too red.

'Nuances, I hear you say!

'Except, Monsieur d'Arlon, the additional nuance is that the red is artificial: it's lipstick.'

'Lipstick?'

'Yes, and not just any: it's from an inhabitant of the estate.

'A trace collected on a handkerchief will confirm it.'

'What are you insinuating?' asked d'Arlon, tense. 'I demand you clarify your accusation.'

'Gladly. When we arrived at that lugubrious cabin, the scent of a very subtle perfume was floating in the air. I detected it clearly and, as a consequence, Triel started his investigations.

'A perfume which you know well, which is very familiar to you, and which may be dear to you...

'Monsieur d'Arlon, I've run out of ways to break the news gently, which I prepared in the Paris-Marseille express: the perfume belongs to Mme. d'Arlon, and the lipstick belongs to Mme. d'Arlon.'

'You're lying,' said d'Arlon, his voice choking.

'Alas, no! I'm not lying. I'm limiting myself to my sad role, which is that of exposing but not explaining. Here is, not *the* truth—for we have yet to peel away the alleged mysteries cluttering up the case—but *a* truth. A fragmentary truth, but an incontestable one.

'Your wife killed Benoît Gérapin.'

'It's not true!'

'Mme. d'Arlon has confessed.'

'Nevertheless....'

'Don't say anything, I beg you.

'Master the beating of your heart, the uncontrolled impulses of your mind. That would be operating in a vacuum.'

You don't know what's behind the words I'm using....

'Could you make an effort for several more minutes, and would you please consider the tragedy as if were fiction, like an unfamiliar game?... It's a Japanese play, acted in masks... Only at the end do the masks come off.'

Horror, fright and incomprehension were written on d'Arlon's face.

'I'll try,' he murmured.

'So, now let's clear up the second of the false mysteries: the apparition in your bedroom.

'We thought we'd reached the climax of the drama in the brief moment when Triel's shot illuminated the scene. Mistake! It was only an episode, more comic than tragic, a conjuring trick partly successful, but partly a failure.

'Question: how could someone have introduced themselves into the bedroom, armed with a bundle of old rags?

'Answer: through the door.'

'Through which door?'

'Through the old arched door, that goes without saying. Ghosts have a strong sense of the picturesque.'

'The bolts weren't drawn.'

'They didn't have to be, my dear sir. That's the nub of it!

'We were all mesmerised by the absurd premise that, to open a door, one must draw the bolts. Mistake!'

'Mistake?'

'Or, rather, omission.

'Even a child can open the most heavily bolted door in the world, *if the housing isn't attached to the door frame!*'

'If the housing... if the door frame...' repeated d'Arlon, who was clearly out of his depth.

'Or, if you prefer, if the iron plate which houses the extremity of the bolt isn't fixed to the wall.

'Now do you understand?'

'Ah!' exclaimed d'Arlon. 'What fools we've all been.'

'Thank you,' I said, 'But please make an exception for Triel, who worked out the trick in one minute, approximately.

'Whilst he was visiting your bedroom—in your company, I think— he had the brilliant idea of touching the wooden screws which attached the iron plate to the frame.

'They turned crazily.

'They were loose, in a cavity too big for them, which had been made for the original screws.'

'So that's it. That little trick enabled anyone in possession of the key to the lock to open the door—a lock well lubricated beforehand, of course.

'The bolt carried the housing with it.

'But unfortunately, the plate fell to the floor with a clatter!'

'Another   mistake. In making that false reasoning, Monsieur d'Arlon, you're assuming our bolt is like other safety bolts.

'But our XIth century bolt is quite different.

'Being of ancient fabrication, it's very solid... The bolt itself, let me remind you, is a rectangular iron bar, of which the plate is the female part. The bar is embedded in the plate and has even rusted inside. It's as one with the plate and carries it along when the door opens.

'Our collective reason almost escaped through that gap.'

*****

'All the incidents of that terrible night are explained by that trick with the door.

'We become skirmishers for the visit to the ground floor. You yourself, in the company of Triel, move with the caution of an Indian through the drawing room, dining room and bedroom.

'Symmetrically, with regard to the corridor, Troubert and Émile explore the kitchen at the same time.

'All the rooms are empty .

'The phantom of Nanteuil, meanwhile, waits patiently at the end of the corridor, hidden in the re-entrant angle defined by the walls of the keep.

'The group d'Arlon-Triel, having accomplished its mission, returns to the corridor.

'If that being had a sense of humour, he must have been in stitches behind the wall which separated him from us.

'And I tend to believe that he had.

'Because, five minutes later, whilst I'm hanging around on the steps of the staircase, he pushes his door open, slips behind me with his silent phantom's step and steals the revolver from my pocket.'

'Do you really think so?'

'There's no other explanation for the disappearance of the revolver.'

D'Arlon will never know the truth about the hands brushing, but he doesn't need to.

'Why did your phantom steal a weapon he didn't use?'

'Maybe he never had the chance to use it. Maybe he was brandishing the revolver in the darkness when Triel fired first.

'But that's not likely. Murder wasn't on the programme for that evening of tightrope walking. Our phantom simply wanted to protect himself against the risk of receiving a bullet.'

'Yes,' said d'Arlon, 'I can see the scene, now. A turn of the key unlocks the door ... Then the hand with the key pushes against the oak panel. The iron plate comes away from the wall, carried by the bolt. The door starts to open....'

'And Triel waits, facing the door....

'He's accepted the duel against the unknown stranger, even in the place where the other plans to surprise him, thanks to a strategy which turns out to be futile.

'He loses at *écarté*. But he has in mind another game, in which he believes he holds invisible trump cards, not counting his revolver, sitting on his knees.

'He holds his cards in his left hand. His right returns to touch the revolver each time he throws away a card.

'And the whole business lasts a matter of seconds. The bundle of rags thrown through the half-open door misses the bullet fired by Triel by seconds.

'The light goes out, but the visitor is wounded. He's the one who's lost.

'He goes back to the dark rectangle from whence he came. He retains enough *sang-froid* to close the door after him. Then re-locks the door.

'When the lighter illuminates the room in Troubert's trembling hand, nothing has changed.

'A single drop of blood on the floor.'

'But that visitor, who was it?'

CHAPTER III

The portrait

'I'm going to withhold the name from you for a few more moments. The name won't help you to understand the affair. Quite the opposite!

'I simply wanted to rid ourselves of the false mysteries obscured by darkness: the death of Gérapin and the apparition of the following night.'

'But behind it there's a real mystery.'

'Yes, and we're getting to that now.

'Monsieur d'Arlon, the tragic-comic interlude of the phantoms is over. And I need your most serious attention once again.

'Can you cast your mind back to the evening in the manor, following Gérapin's death?

'You described your life, your engagement, your marriage, your return....

'Opposite you sat three newcomers, still wrapped up in coats and scarves, their shoes still covered with mud from the park, listening to your very lucid account. They were asking themselves what part you played in the drama in the cabin... And if the ringleader of the show wasn't actually you.

'You brought, by way of justification, letters from your fiancée and letters from your wife. We looked at them distractedly, paying more attention to your voice than to the papers from which , seemingly, you wished to divert our attention.

'And the first light went on.

'I'm not talking about the yellow light, of which the Nanteuil lamps seem to have the exclusivity. I'm talking about an intellectual illumination which would strike those amongst us best equipped to receive it.'

'Your friend Triel, obviously?'

'Our friend Triel, obviously.

'Specifically, it seems that the letters from Mlle.de Nanteuil *were not written in exactly the same hand as those from your wife.*'

Having pronounced this crucially important sentence, I waited for the reaction.

D'Arlon merely shrugged his shoulders.

'Forgive me,' he said, 'but your intellectual illumination doesn't dazzle me.'

'Very well,' I said. 'I shall dot the i's.

'In the chest you placed on the table there were two categories of letter. Those which Jeanne de Nanteuil addressed to you from France, and those which Mme. d'Arlon addressed to you from Saigon, during your tours of inspection.

'Isn't that so?'

'You seem fixated on the titles "Mme." and "Mlle.,"' said d'Arlon. 'Marriage, which changes the names of women, doesn't, as far as I know, change their handwriting.'

'I believe it doesn't, in general. However, in this case it did.'

D'Arlon looked at me blankly. Plainly, he didn't see where I was headed.

'And what conclusion did your friend draw from this fact?' he asked eventually.

'He didn't draw a conclusion. But he permitted himself to formulate a hypothesis. A strange hypothesis—one might even say romantic. But a plausible one, and one which explains the colour of the wallpaper in the Fougeras' bedroom.'

D'Arlon said with a start:

'What? What's this about wallpaper?'

'Listen to me, I beg of you. By the way, you're free to go to Nanteuil and see for yourself.

'Go into the Fougeras' bedroom. Look up at the wall above the chest of drawers. The wallpaper there—in deplorable taste, I agree—is mauve with rose garlands. A crucifix supports a branch of box.

'Now, adjacent to the crucifix to the left, the paper shines more brightly than elsewhere. Over a surface area of about thirty centimetres square, the roses are fresher and their leaves are greener.'

'A miracle? The influence of the crucifix?'

'More likely that of an old frame that had hung for a long time in that spot.

'You must have seen empty rooms after everything has been moved out. Where the furniture and pictures have protected the walls from the light, the paper is less "faded," as they say.'

'Obviously.'

'The statement is self-evident. But a psychological seed will fertilize it.

'We peasants. Monsieur d'Arlon, don't like moving things, that's just a fact. The wedding photograph of cousin Jules, hung from a nail in a cheap frame, is there for the eternity.

'Many houses in Marly still carry, washed by the rain, the wooden panel, on which was carved the number of officers, men, and horses they took in during the war..

'Why did the Fougeras remove the picture frame next to the crucifix?

'Don't shrug your shoulders, Monsieur d'Arlon! The whole mystery of Nanteuil is there!

'According to Triel's enquiries, the wallpaper was put up seven years ago. The frame wasn't there then, as can be verified from the old layer.

'The frame was hung later, but it's difficult to know exactly when.

'It was taken down about two years ago.

'For what reason? And what became of it?'

'You're asking yourself questions,' said d'Arlon. 'Please be good enough to reply to yourself!'

'That's what I'm about to do, but I wanted you to follow Triel's train of thought about a picture which had been removed, but perhaps not destroyed....

'When to visit the Fougeras' lodge, occupied day and night by the two concierges?

'During Gérapin's funeral. That was the second occasion—and the last.

'And that's why Triel disappeared during part of the ceremony.

'When he rejoined the procession, at the cemetery gate, his hands blackened by the dust in the attic he'd just searched, he knew what was the mystery of Nanteuil.'

'Perhaps,' said d'Arlon, 'you might eventually get to the point?'

'Here it is.'

I took two photographs out of my pocket.

I handed him the first.

'The portrait which had hung on the wall?'

'Yes.'

It was the face of a young woman, enlarged by a crude operator. Fifteen years old, perhaps. Brown hair pulled back and tied clumsily in a chignon. But, despite the poor coiffure and the vulgarity of the image, the face was attractive, touched with finesse and gentleness.

Very attractive, no doubt, because d'Arlon couldn't take his eyes off it... Because he turned his chair round to catch the light from the window.

'Who is she?' he asked.

'The snapshot lacks clarity,' I said. 'Understandably: it's an enlargement.

'Nevertheless, with a magnifying glass, you can make out a name, in the lower left corner: Élise Fougeras.'

'The concierges' daughter?'

'Yes.'

'I don't remember having seen her at Nanteuil, during my rare visits.'

He continued to stare at the photograph.

'There's something rather unusual,' he said with difficulty, passing his hand across his brow.

'Here,' I said, 'let's finish this.'

And I handed him the second photo.

He took it with his left hand, keeping the other in his right hand. He compared them carefully.

'The second portrait,' he said slowly, 'is just a retouch of the first, I believe?'

'Exactly. An artistic work from the hand of Triel.'

'I can tell. The coiffure has been modified. The hair has been cut and waved according to modern style. The eyebrows are finer...

'The mouth seems smaller. A simple question of make-up.'

He returned to the first image and dreamt for a moment, apparently talking to himself.

'A few extra years on the young face to make it thinner and finer... To make it more guarded, more secret... Shades of anxiety, perhaps ambition... The sheen of luxury as well... And *voilà*.'

Suddenly remembering my presence, he looked up at me with eyes flecked with yellow, once again the exasperated and unrestrained d'Arlon I had confronted before.

'I see, Monsieur Dutheil, that, during the retouching, the name in the lower left corner, Élise Fougeras, was removed.'

'Yes.'

'Why fail to add in its place the name that obviously comes to mind: Jeanne d'Arlon?'

*****

I didn't say a word. I became suddenly conscious, from the change in his expression, of having wounded this man too deeply. I would have preferred to defer the end of the explanation, for *the worst had not yet been said.*

But d'Arlon, who would not take his eyes off me, and drawing himself up to his full height, was looking for the final blow.

With a gesture that was not even violent, he cast the two photographs on the table, renouncing at the same time both Jeanne d'Arlon and Élise Fougeras.

'Never speak of this woman again,' he said. 'She has betrayed me, she has killed... I want to expunge even her memory.

'Just one question, sir. I became engaged, two years ago, to Mlle. de Nanteuil.

'Where is my fiancée?'

'How do I know?'I said. 'She is no more...

'Her body has contrived to be lost, near here, *somewhere in the waters of the old port....*'

CHAPTER IV

Confrontation

The sound of voices suddenly filled the room. The approach of noon emptied the contents of a nearby school into the street. Chatter, cries, shouts, laughter. A tram rang its bell persistently beneath the window, no doubt in order to make a way through the crowd. It continued on its way with a metallic rattle as the infantile crowd dispersed.

D'Arlon mechanically stroked his left and right cheeks and reassured himself that he'd shaved. He checked his neck, which was bare, and then the collar of his shirt, which was open.

He got up and busied himself completing his toilet.

There was something automatic about his gestures. They made me think of a dog I'd once seen in a Paris street, which had been run over by a car, but was licking its wounds and still trying to move forward.

'Are you leaving?' I asked.

'Yes.'

'Where are you going?'

'Home.'

'Home?'

'Yes... To Saigon.'

All the desperate efforts with the collar and the bourgeois respectability were both touching and risible.

What was less risible was d'Arlon's aged face. The wardrobe mirror reflected that of a fifty-year-old man.

'Believe me, I sympathise with your—.'

'You,' said d'Arlon, cutting me off with a concentrated fury, 'are a scoundrel.'

So much for breaking the news gently.

'You're wallowing in these sordid stories, you and your friends,' continued d'Arlon, looking for his collar button on the mantelpiece. 'Good for you. Enjoy yourselves!

'I haven't got the same tastes.'

135

'I note that you won't even let me expose….'

'Not a word more. I've already heard too much for the peace and quiet which will be my future life.

'Everything disgusts me, and everyone, including you.'

'And the fate of the young woman who shared your life for more than a year doesn't interest you at all?'

'I repeat for the last time that I don't know that woman!' exclaimed d'Arlon, his features distorted by rage. 'May that impostor, daughter of concierges and a two-time criminal never be mentioned again!'

His hands were trembling so badly he had to restart tying his knot three times.

After which he put on his jacket, looked down his nose at me and repeated:

'I'm leaving.'

When I saw that he did indeed intend to leave and drop everything, my patience snapped.

'Go,' I said. 'But you will remember what I'm going to say, Monsieur d'Arlon: pride and bitter disappointment are making you commit a cowardly act.'

D'Arlon stopped dead. I believe he would have thrown furniture at me, if he'd had the strength. His bird-of-prey eyes were burning.

'What did you just say?'

'What's the point of repeating it? From now on, your conscience will remind you of my words.'

And, after another of his menacing gestures, which got me really worked up, I shouted:

'He who refuses to listen to the truth is afraid.'

He tried to quieten me, but I was in full flight:

'So, leave!' I said. 'You're right. We've seen more than enough of you. We knew we were giving all we had for a mediocre and infatuated being. Triel said so again yesterday. For such a puppet!

'What panic when we come to threaten him in his place of residence with an effort of intelligence and comprehension. His hand goes to his false collar as if it were armour. We shed a little light on the life he's led up to now. He runs away to the other side of the world.'

'Monsieur Dutheil!'

'Look at yourself in the mirror, you and your false collar. You're as pale as each other now.

'What role could you two play in this complex drama? You don't even know how to hold your own in *Loved by his Concierge.'*

'Monsieur Dutheil!'

'What,' I said, 'are you still here? Why?

'We don't need you, Triel and I. It is we who are your liquidators.

'It is we, Monsieur René d'Arlon, who will decide the fate of your wife. It is we, Monsieur René d'Arlon, who will punish the murderers of your fiancée!

'And if we can't, alas! build a sepulchre for the sacrificed body of Jeanne d'Arlon, at least we will, in your name, throw a few flowers on her liquid grave.'

Beads of perspiration had appeared on d'Arlon's forehead.

I stopped, out of breath from the violence of my words.

We looked at each other in silence.

Somewhere, an invisible referee banged a gong and announced "Time!"

D'Arlon pulled up a chair and forgot to offer me another.

'So, speak,' he said. 'I'm listening.'

*****

Eventually, after a confrontation lasting half an hour, during which I had lost and regained contact with my impossible listener, I considered my goal had been achieved.

The most terrible had been said. All that remained was for me to explain and the morality would follow naturally.

'Cigarette?'

'Please.'

The gestures of presenting a cigarette case and offering a light are precious, in certain circumstances. They re-establish human intercourse. The first puffs of smoke rise in a calmer atmosphere.

Thus I continued my narrative in a more relaxed manner than hitherto.

'The instigator of this whole business,' I said, 'must no doubt be known to you already....'

137

CHAPTER V

Another portrait

'Benoît Gérapin, Mme. d'Arlon told us on the tragic night when we first made her acquaintance, was the jack-of-all-trades of the estate. He could do everything, certainly—and more besides!

'I invited you just now to look at the panorama of Nanteuil ten years ago. If we had been more perceptive, we would have detected, above the lawns, above the tall trees and above the manor, a delicate web spun by the spider Gérapin.

'I'm not privy to his earlier manoeuvres. But it was certainly because of him that fear and anxiety pervaded the paths and alleyways for such a long time.

'The two solitary women sensed the existence of an ill-defined menace. That was why the elder Mme. de Nanteuil had the walls built higher and replaced the locks. All to no avail... the enemy was already within.

'Her daughter was warned in turn. More than once, a step other than hers had caused dead branches to crack, in that corner of the park where she carried her boredom around with her. More than once, she thought she saw a shape pass beneath her window at night.

'But Gérapin never decided to attempt the act of violence which was obsessing him on the young girl, which would probably have ruined his ambitions rather than crown them.

'The months go by. Mlle. de Nanteuil becomes engaged, accepting one of the first suitors to propose, no disrespect intended.

'At that moment, her old mother suddenly dies.'

D'Arlon was following my narrative with rapt attention. He could not help interrupting me.

'Did that death, under the circumstances...'

'...take on a new significance?

'It's an obvious question. But there's nothing to indicate it did.

'Be that as it may, crime or coincidence, the result is not what Gérapin had a right to expect.

'Jeanne de Nanteuil finds herself at his mercy, but she gets away...
She leaves and is going to join you.

'Is everything lost?

'No. Everything is won.

'You already know Gérapin's hideous response.

'Jeanne de Nanteuil leaves the manor, but it's Élise Fougeras who arrives in Saigon. Élise Fougeras, Gérapin's cousin.'

'His accomplice!'

'Maybe not to the degree you think.'

D'Arlon dismissed the question with a wave of his hand.

'There's one thing inexplicable in your theory,' he said.

'According to you, there were two adolescents living in Nanteuil at the same time: the daughter of the family and the daughter of the concierge.

'And their resemblance was such that one could be substituted for the other?'

'Listen,' I said. 'There may be a simple explanation: a very simple one.

'I haven't researched the matter, but I've heard tales about Gontran de Nanteuil, Jeanne's father... In fact, maybe you knew the gentleman?'

'No, he died in 1905. His portrait hangs in the drawing room, above the mantelpiece.'

'I've seen it. Broad shoulders, full blond beard, ruddy face, military bearing.

'Tell me, what memory does the family have of him?'

'An unfavourable one. If Mme. de Nanteuil had known misery, if she had spent the last twenty years of her life in isolation, it was partly because of this man. A wastrel and a libertine.'

'In the region, he was known more bluntly as a womanizer.

'Now, all this was happening whilst Marthe Fougeras, the concierge's wife, was a fresh young creature.

'So that, my God....

'Élise Fougeras and Jeanne de Nanteuil did have a similar look about them, it's true. The features they had in common could perhaps be found in the portrait in the drawing room?'

'That's certainly one explanation,' said d'Arlon, in surprise.

'In any case, it's only of secondary importance.'

'No importance whatsoever!'

It seemed to me that, on the contrary, d'Arlon had greeted the news favourably. That he married beneath him became less certain. What a mess!

I had to return to my painful subject.

'We were talking about Élise Fougeras' participation in Gérapin's machinations. It seems as though the young woman was another who was disgracefully manipulated.

'Eight days before her departure to Marseille, Mlle. de Nanteuil received a visit from Old Fougeras. He came to tell her of his intention not to keep Élise in Nanteuil. She was unhappy there. She was going to be useless, having up to now been assigned to service in the manor.

'The Fougeras had relatives in Bogny, in Burgundy, who owned a large farm. Young Élise would be happy there. She would easily find a suitable match....

'A suitable match! The old peasant could scarcely conceal the gleam in his eye as he pronounced the words.

'Jeanne de Nanteuil agreed. Particularly since that would reduce the running costs of the estate.

'Élise Fougeras leaves Nanteuil. A convenient indisposition prevents her mother from accompanying her. Not to worry! Benoît Gérapin is there to replace her—but he doesn't take her to Burgundy....

'Two days later, Jeanne leaves through the wrought iron gate.

'And, a few days after that, Benoît Gérapin returns alone...'

CHAPTER VI

The manoeuvre

'Come over to the window, Monsieur d'Arlon. Can you make out, to the right, the line of grey roofs which makes one think of the grim towns of the Pas-de-Calais transported to the heart of Marseille?

'Two dramas played out there simultaneously, which decided the fates of two young women.

'Both were wrapped in mists and shrouds. Marseille, in that month of December, melted into shadow at five o'clock in the evening.

'Concerning the act which sent Jeanne de Nanteuil into dark and icy waters, we will never know anything. The murderer finished as suddenly as his victim. Neither one nor the other had time to utter a cry.

'Concerning the evening Élise Fougeras and Benoît Gérapin passed together afterwards, it's not much easier to shine a light. The survivor, who could have been a witness, remained as tight-lipped as a dead woman on the subject. For Triel, determined to get to the truth, it required all his ardour and, almost, his violence.

'Can you put yourself in the place of the young girl, who had never left her home in Marly, carried along a ribbon of railway a thousand kilometres long?

'The names of the unfamiliar places which flash past... the evening that falls on the hills and, after a fitful sleep, the dawn of a new day with the journey still not over...

'And the silence of the disquieting companion sitting next to her on the wooden bench of a third-class compartment....

'At last, a big station full of smoke: Marseille.

'"We have to hide," whispers Gérapin, during the brouhaha of the arrival... "The police are after us."

'And he shows her a letter written by her father, telling her to follow her cousin's instructions precisely.

'The young woman, paralysed by fear, allows herself to be bundled into a taxi. Houses and pedestrians flash past, as if in a bad dream.

143

'Then it's confinement in a room in a seedy hotel.

'Gérapin has left after promising her:

'"This evening, everything will be sorted out."

'And he's locked her in.

'Even then, the young girl hesitates for fear of scandal. But she vows to get a proper explanation from her cousin.

'Towards nightfall, Gérapin returns, as promised. He brings along a suitcase she doesn't recognise.

'The next day, Élise Fougeras boards *l'Aquitaine* under the name of Jeanne de Nanteuil.'

'Willingly, it would appear?'

'Monsieur d'Arlon, don't condemn her yet. You're still suffering from the blow to your self-esteem.'

'On the contrary, I'm considering the matter with complete objectivity.'

'Too much objectivity, and not enough human understanding. You're passing judgment on an eighteen-year-old child who's been abducted and violated.

'There's no doubt Gérapin fooled her. He invented a romantic story wherein Jeanne de Nanteuil, having fallen in love with someone else, was the real instigator of the substitution.

'But even when Élise Fougeras senses the truth, in other words, the crime, what can she do about it? The ones who set her up for this venture were her own parents, which means she has no one in the world she can turn to.

'And if she says anything, it will send Gérapin to the scaffold and her parents to jail. A terrible situation, to which I direct your disinterested attention!

'Moreover, she's afraid of Gérapin, dreadfully afraid... The killer doesn't leave her side. He knows how to keep her quiet, if need be. He's already done it once....

'He accompanies her to the boat. She boards in a kind of daze, firmly held by the arm. Below her gleam the waters which have already received the body of Jeanne de Nanteuil...

'Walking the gangplank of *l'Aquitaine* is an ordeal.

'Yet that is her only crime.'

D'Arlon doesn't say a word.

'You were surprised, after that, that your fiancée had shown such little interest in her grand voyage. Port Said, Djibouti, Colombo, all go unnoticed by that child. On the return trip, she seemed to be seeing them for the first time.

'In reality, she had never seen them!

'She had remained locked in her cabin. The terror of the departure did not dissipate until the terror of the arrival. Every hour of that silence, with the engines humming below, weakened her. On the gangplank of *l'Aquitaine* she was still a victim. In Saigon, she would be an accomplice!

'Thus, the farther she distances herself from Gérapin, the tighter her ties to the murderer become. It is a veritable running knot which he has placed around her neck.

'*And she will do the same to him...*'

CHAPTER VII

A rope around the neck

'Thus it was that you saw a young girl dressed in black disembark, whose paleness, silence and red eyes frightened you. You no longer recognised your fiancée. It must be said there were several reasons for that.

'In fact, the mourning clothes lent some credence to her grief.

'Time went by. And time heals many things.

'A few months later, your wedding took place in Saigon.'

I paused.

D'Arlon remained expressionless.

'Élise Fougeras, now your wife, tries desperately to forget. She would have succeeded, no doubt, if you had not been so insistent on returning to France....

'Meanwhile, at the other end of the world, Benoît Gérapin is getting impatient. He senses that his victim is trying to escape. At his suggestion, Old Fougeras sends you intriguing letters, remarkably calibrated, which further increase your desire to see Nanteuil again.

'And, one beautiful evening, you yourself deliver Benoît Gérapin's prey to him.'

Continued silence from d'Arlon.

'From that point on, with the park gate closed behind the groups of antagonists, a tragedy was inevitable. There had to be a victim.

'There was every chance, sir, that the victim would be you.

'Thanks to your wife, it was someone else....

'The battle is preceded by an argument between Mme. d'Arlon and Benoît Gérapin. The wretch had worked out that the woman he had believed would be his accomplice had changed sides. He demands to meet her, he threatens her, he promises her things could become unpleasant.

'Mme. d'Arlon, who finds herself caught between her cousin and her husband—a position as comfortable as being held by pincers—yields. She still hopes to play the role of an intermediary.

147

'The meeting takes place in a deserted corner of the park at twilight. Your wife speaks first. She begs, she offers money and jewels. She promises to arrange that you never to come back to Nanteuil. The property will effectively belong to the Fougeras. That's their objective isn't it?

'At which point Gérapin removes the mask completely. She's right about Nanteuil. Let the old people have it.

'He has grander plans. The luck of the game has placed several trump cards in his hand. He plays them now.

'In a word, you, Monsieur d'Arlon, will not leave the manor alive. That's a given.

'Your widow, who, let us not forget, inherits not only the Nanteuil estate, but also the Kay mines, will return to Indochina to take care of affairs and liquidate them.

'She will take with her a trusted companion, energetic and resourceful, who will be only too happy to help her defend her interests: Benoît Gérapin.

'And, further down the road, there will be nothing to prevent him from marrying her.

'As you can see, this gardener's son should have been born in XVth century Italy. He murders some, takes others by force, as well as their riches, and eliminates husbands as negligible factors.

'Your wife listens to all that as if in a nightmare.

'She wants to leave, but he grabs her by her wrists.

'"Don't forget who you are… And you're already complicit in what happened in Marseille."

'She feels faint and dares not call out. Gérapin knows that he's the stronger, the winner.

'So, to seal the union, and to celebrate it at the same time, Gérapin seizes her in his arms and takes her away from the meeting spot.'

I pause to take note of d'Arlon's paleness and the slight trembling of his hands, resting on his knees.

So, my good man, is this story all news to you?

'The undergrowth is soaking wet. No matter. Gérapin knows there's a small cabin conveniently located less than fifty metres away.

'He takes his barely conscious victim there, carrying her in his arms like a baby. His clogs make deep footprints in the wet clay.

'He props her up against a partition wall. Then he locks them both

148

inside. He puts the key in his pocket. He takes off his jacket, which he folds carefully. All done as calmly as if he'd just brought a girl into a hotel room.

'She, meanwhile, regains consciousness. Her eyes dilate in the darkness. She knows very well what's going to happen, and the physical stain which will precede the moral ones, then more complete possession—an entire ignoble cycle in which she is already engaged.

'Then....

'Then the narrative becomes difficult to construct with precision.

'All of that, your wife has explained to Triel. But she herself has only the confused memory of a moment of dizziness....

'During his preparations, she has been clinging tightly to one of the ropes hanging from the rafters. Rough old ropes with which, not long ago, she tied bundles of firewood.

'How was it that her fingers found the familiar form of a running knot?

'Was it meant for her, in order to end it all?

'Already the man was advancing, hands outstretched before him. He was unable to see, in the darkness, a circle of rope hanging in front of the woman's face, like the frame of a portrait.

'His hands were searching for her loins, his lips sought her lips and found them...

'But he hadn't counted on the sudden explosion of murderous rage, the victim's leap as she literally threw herself at him and clung to him... He staggered under the unexpected shock... He fell, with all the woman's weight hanging from his shoulders....

'There was a dry crack, like that of a dead branch. It was already over.'

CHAPTER VIII

The double footprint

'What is truly remarkable in this story is not the summary execution, but the ten minutes which followed.

'The Lord knows there have been enough women subject to furious surges of anger, sometimes even leading to murder. But afterwards they faint, flee madly down the stairs, or bring out the neighbours.

'Your wife initially behaved like the others, that's to say she shook the locked door desperately, bruised her fists on the partition wall, and filled the shed with despairing cries.

'She found herself stretched out on the floor, sobbing nervously.

'After which, if she did not want to spend the night in the cabin, she had to collect her thoughts.

'Benoît Gérapin, sagging at the end of the rope like a broken marionette, his head to one side and his knees folded in two, swung gently from side to side.

'A sinister face-to-face.

'Others would have begun to panic. Élise Fougeras pulled herself together. She got up, searched the dead man's hot pockets, and removed the key. An immense effort, in which the murderous reflex of a few minutes earlier paled by comparison.

'Then she opened the door.

'A gust of cold air struck her in the face and brought her to her senses. The Marly church clock struck half-past seven. Only twenty minutes had elapsed since meeting Benoît in the park.

'At that moment, you were travelling peacefully towards Nanteuil. The Fougeras were dipping their spoons in their bowls of soup. Joséphine was setting the table in the manor dining room.

'Everything was calm, all around.

'And so it was necessary to break that circle of peace and stir up scandal... Why, why, for God's sake, when the only culprit had already been punished?

'In the moonlight, the footprints of Gérapin's clogs were clearly

151

visible.

'Tomorrow, at this same spot, policemen crowding round the young woman would be asking why she allowed herself to be transported across the park in the arms of her gardener…And why he had started to undress her inside the shed….

'The questioning wouldn't stop there. They would investigate the private lives of all the manor guests. And, some day, Jeanne de Nanteuil's ghost would arise from the waters of the old port… The horror of it!

'What to do?

'That set of accusatory footprints in the mud….

'It was whilst she was contemplating them, in a sort of overwhelmed stupor, that your wife sensed the idea of salvation stir within her.

'Yes, there was a way to save the situation. Just one way. All it took was courage.

'And so: your wife goes back into the shed. She approaches Gérapin for the second time. She moves the table out of the corner. She finds the force to lift the body, sit it on the table and steady it.

'Then she loosens the running knot.

'The knot higher up, around the rafter, is too difficult to untie; we proved that together.

'Mme. d'Arlon doesn't touch it. Instead, she throws the end of the rope over the rafter a few times, in order to shorten the length of the free rope.

'After which, *she hangs Gérapin for the second time.*

'She does it by moving the table to one side, so that the feet of the hanged man swing slightly above the floor.

'It's pretty astonishing, I have to say. Not everyone is capable of executing the same person twice. And, by the way, this episode confirms my hunch that your wife has the blood of the Nanteuils running in her veins. She fearlessly exercised her right of higher justice on the peasant Benoît Gérapin.

'The objective of this staging is evident. To prevent anyone imagining the real crime. To make them think it must be suicide. For, as someone observed, to hang someone as heavy as Gérapin above his own height would require an entire team of executioners.

'Now it's done. Everything is in order.

'Mme. d'Arlon departs, leaving only the trace of her light perfume.'

'But how does she leave?'

'Oh, just like everyone else: on foot.

'The only precaution she takes is to place her delicate feet, in their narrow shoes, inside the huge footprints made by Gérapin's clogs.

'A body destined for his caresses made the kidnapper's arms heavier on the way in.

'What weight of remorse presses on that young woman who returns alone in the dark with strides that are too slow and too long?

'Already, dampness is oozing from the soaking wet ground. A fine drizzle begins. It's more than enough to mask the second set of footprints.

'And, the following day, I shall be asking myself if Triel hasn't got a screw loose, when he goes to test the temperature of the puddles of water with his finger.'

CHAPTER IX

The woman in mourning

'The incidents of the following night were secondary. Even though, at the time, we held a very different opinion!

'With Gérapin eliminated from the field of operations, and Triel still on the side of the spectators, the stage is only occupied by two second-rate actors.

'On the one hand, Old Fougeras' failed attempt to seize the rudder abandoned by Gérapin.

'On the other hand, a procession —equally failed—prompted by your wife.

'In brief, a duel of the inept.

'A spectator of goodwill judges the final. Triel, with one gesture, ensures the defeat of Old Fougeras, who had been convinced he was winning on points.'

'I don't follow you,' says d'Arlon. 'Could you use less colourful language, please! So the phantom of the bedroom was Old Fougeras?'

'Assuredly! The old man had good cards in his hands and he played them.

'He knew one essential detail, the rigging of the bedroom door, through which Gérapin was supposed to come one night, which would have been your last.

'How Gérapin was planning to kill you without being suspected is a secret of that strange soul, prematurely departed.

'But he had hinted to your wife that a spring had been wound up against you, and she sensed that it could still be released, despite the disappearance of its creator.

'She leads you along.

'You flee—reluctantly, but you flee.

'Old Fougeras tries his luck and blocks the gate.

'First round to Old Fougeras!

'But the second round looks more difficult.

'Troubert, Triel and I have been trapped in Nanteuil, thus

increasing the number of the besieged.

'And Old Fougeras has to act that very night.

'So it was that we were all huddled together like frightened sheep. Despite your recriminations, Monsieur d'Arlon, I'm reminding you. In the circumstances, all your efforts tended to lead you to lie down in the coffin carefully prepared for you by Benoît Gérapin. And your history is one of permanent rescue.'

D'Arlon shoots me a furious look and says tersely:

'It's possible.'

'It's quite certain!'

I continue:

'You remember as well as I do—and for just as long—the incidents which occurred that night. Old Fougeras is completely at home in the manor. And he operates with a surprising dexterity and lightness of touch.

'First he covers himself against major risk by stealing Troubert's revolver from me by using the sealed door, which opens behind my back.

'And, with the same ease, he then pushes us from the dining room into your bedroom.

'After which, although his victims are caught in a trap, he doesn't dare confront them. There are too many mice in the mousetrap!

'I believe, in the silence of the XIth century staircase, that Old Fougeras abandons Gérapin's murderous projects, which, moreover, have lost their sense and impact.

'What he wants is to make a grand gesture. To bring our terror, which is undeniable, to a climax.

'After such a night, Nanteuil will be free of all of us and left to the ghosts. Old Fougeras will become the master, in fact, if not by right.

'And so, he proceeds to carry out the acts according to his nephew's plan.

'He sabotages the electricity. He opens the sealed door. With a steady hand, he throws the bunch of rags and hits the chandelier.

'And he would have succeeded in his efforts, had he not had as his adversary, at the other side of the table, our friend Stéphane Triel.

'It wasn't a fair match!'

*****

156

'But why did Triel let him escape, after he caught the other red-handed?'

'And why didn't Triel have Mme. d'Arlon arrested the night before, after she confessed to the murder?

'Because our amateur friend isn't paid at a piece rate and wasn't in any particular hurry.

'He sensed that, in the drama of Nanteuil, there was something more than the settling of scores by two former lovers. He wanted to work it all out for himself—in his own way, which is discreetly.

'And that earned him, by way of a dusty portrait, and whilst Gérapin's hearse slowly advanced, the special joy: that of the final verification.

'He had confided in me once that it was right that Truth should be represented by the body of a beautiful woman. To conquer her and denude her is sometimes quick. More often it is long and risky. But, in either case, there comes a moment which rewards all the effort—and much more.

'Gérapin's coffin had just reached the grave which had been dug for it when Triel rejoined us.

'The family assembled around the muddy hole.

'The family, Monsieur d'Arlon! Your family by dint of marrying beneath you. Do you remember them?

'Not particularly, needless to say. You were thinking of other things besides those concierges. Of your wife, perhaps....

'And the woman's sobs which could be heard only served to increase your malaise.

'You extended a hand absent-mindedly to the grief-stricken parents.

'Triel followed after you...

'What things, Monsieur d'Arlon, can be conveyed by a simple handshake! The basic contact is an exchange of fluids. I believe there's even a special gift, which we could call handshake sensitivity.

'Except, Monsieur d'Arlon, you are devoid of it, to a remarkable degree.

'You didn't notice, in Old Fougeras' handshake, a shiver, a withdrawal? Triel noticed it. It's true that he probably shook it vigorously—that bandaged hand beneath the black glove. The hand he'd put a bullet through the previous night.

'And the next hand... I'll wager that it didn't register with you, either.'

'I don't remember. Whose was it?'

'Come, come, Monsieur d'Arlon... after the two Fougeras... A third and final person... That woman hidden beneath the mourning veil, who couldn't suppress her sobbing...'

'...?'

'Why, their daughter, their only daughter! Élise Fougeras!'

CHAPTER X

René d'Arlon

It was already long past midday.

The sun, having turned, now inundated the room. The noise from the streets and the hubbub within the hotel had subsided. And there was an odour rising from the kitchen, the odour of garlic cooking.

My narrative must have lasted more than two hours, interrupted only by the starts and angry outbursts of my listener.

But now d'Arlon remained still, thunderstruck by my last revelation.

'But what was she doing there,' he said, 'next to that wretch's coffin?'

'For heaven's sake!' I replied, 'because that was the only place where she had nothing to fear from the inspectors of the *Sûreté*, even though there was one in attendance!

'For Jeanne d'Arlon, alone and without help, watched for at all the stations—for Jeanne d'Arlon, whose husband may very well have thrown her out if she'd told him the truth—the only refuge was the Fougeras' lodge.'

'Couldn't she have stayed next to me and said nothing?'

'She couldn't, not with the police jumping up and down, and in need of a culprit! Troubert would eventually have thought of collecting the souvenirs of the young Élise Fougeras and asking the parents for the address of the Burgundy farm.

'Besides, the daughter's absence from her cousin's funeral would have been noticed....

'There was no other way to do it.

'There's no doubt that, by disappearing, she took responsibility for all the crimes. But she led the police along a trail which left Nanteuil and got lost far, far away from there.

'She did leave.

'On a real voyage, by the way, from the manor to the lodge: an entire life to go back on.'

'Yes,' said d'Arlon. 'I understand everything, now. And her strange expression when you saw her midway....'

*****

The silence continued.

The story was finished, but no one tried to conclude it.

What was d'Arlon thinking? What had he decided?

'Now you understand,' I say, to break the silence, 'what Triel meant when he called it the most beautiful burial of his life.

'All the actors come back to take their bow when the curtain falls, clad in various accessories: black cotton gloves, crepe veils, deal coffin.

'At the time, no one recognises them.

'A complete denouement, at which nobody recognises anything.'

D'Arlon's wandering thoughts seemed to seize on those last words.

'A complete denouement, you're right.'

He thought for a few moments. Or, rather, he was looking for and weighing his words.

'When all's said and done,' he said, 'there was a crime, and the crime was punished.

'There was a deception, which resolved itself, I think?'

He paused.

My eyes never left his face. I couldn't help but finish for him:

'I believe I understand you. Benoît Gérapin , in the Marly cemetery and Élise Fougeras, in her parents' lodge, both finally found their rightful place.

'And when you find yours again in Saigon, order will have been restored.

'Won't it?

'Isn't that what you meant to say?'

D'Arlon didn't reply.

The sun was making a dazzling circle on the waxed parquet floor. D'Arlon's eyes, shrinking from the glare, remained fixed on mine. It was as if he were expecting something more. But what?

I felt a rising bitterness. So much effort and so many words to arrive at this point, at the sad and gloomy conclusion I was anticipating.

Say something, my friend! If you don't want to show pity for her, don't expect me to show pity for you.

'Knowing that you prefer your denouements complete,' I said, 'there's something you should know.

'Élise Fougeras—well, the woman you no longer know by that name—is going to die.'

D'Arlon's eyes remained firmly shut. As a result of what sentiment?

'You won't have to carry that image with you, Monsieur d'Arlon. So much the better for you!

'As for me, I saw your wife that evening, pale, in her humble mourning clothes, her hair tied in a bun at the back of the neck, sitting on the stone bench in front of the entrance to the lodge.

'Was she Élise Fougeras or Jeanne d'Arlon? The two images merge and become blurred.

'The shadows of the two miserable beings in the lodge paced back and forth in front of the lighted window. The trees in the park murmured stories about Mlle. de Nanteuil and Benoît Gérapin.

'What she was thinking, I do not know.

'But her thin face spoke for her, she who never uttered a complaint.

'I hope for your peace of mind, Monsieur d'Arlon, that her shadow is as soft and silent as you remember it.'

Not a word. He couldn't find anything to say!

The only nerve I ever touched within him was pride.

It is I who am at the end of my tether, not he!

I get up.

He follows me with his eyes.

'Why did you do all this?'

'Certainly not for the love of you.'

'For the love of my wife, then?'

'Yes… It would have been wonderful to have saved her, despite herself and despite everything.

'Triel played his part well. I failed in mine.'

'Don't reproach yourself,' says d'Arlon. 'You've been a bit disorganised, perhaps, but very convincing and very moving, I can assure you.'

He dares! He dares to make fun of me, at such a moment!

'In this affair,' he continues, blithely unaware, 'we meet all the traditional characters of a detective novel. There's the amateur detective, who dabbles a little, shoots blind, and then keeps quiet. His intervention, needless to say, is crucial. There's the faithful confidant, who doesn't understand much, but who is pleasant and verbose. There's a sinister knave, a family of sordid peasants, a pure young woman....

'And then there's an imbecile: me.'

That sudden convergence of our thoughts stuns me for a moment, and I ask myself if I've heard correctly.

But d'Arlon, frowning, insists:

'And when I say imbecile, I'm being polite. In the role that I've played, the odious is matched only by the ridiculous. That's your opinion, too, isn't it?'

'It was, up until a minute ago.'

'Stick to it. It's the right one!'

He displays the furious manner of his worst days.

He's speaking in his usual curt manner, but his voice starts to quiver when he asks:

'You say that Jeanne's life is in danger?'

So! Now he's given up his secret.

*****

My look says clearly:

'Imbecile! I knew you loved her!'

But my lips say:

'I'm not a doctor, as you know. I just gave you my impression.'

D'Arlon stands up and asks me:

'Will you take me to her?'

I've been waiting for that question for three hours!

I reply immediately:

'Impossible.'

'Impossible? Why?'

'I told you just now that I didn't know exactly where your wife was. And that's the truth, Monsieur d'Arlon.'

Come on! Don't keep him in suspense any longer.

'She's in Arles or in Tarascon... Closer, perhaps, if Triel put his foot to the pedal... Farther, if he's had a flat tyre.'

162

'What are you saying? Triel is bringing her here?'

'Yes. An abduction, of sorts, but to your benefit.'

He stares hard at me.

'You've done that, *as well?*'

'We don't do things by halves.'

'What about the police?'

'That's all been arranged. Troubert knows everything.'

D'Arlon's face darkens.

'Troubert knows everything—and then some.

'He knows the identity of the phantom the other night. He worked out the sealed door trick.

'Better yet: he knows about Mme. d'Arlon's abduction by the Fougeras family.'

'What do you mean?'

'Don't you know , Monsieur d'Arlon, that your wife was held for a week in a concealed room in the concierge's lodge?

'Engrave it in your mind, for it is officially the key to the Nanteuil affair.'

'What do I need to understand?'

'You need to understand this, which Inspector Troubert only discovered after a lengthy investigation, with the aid of Triel and myself: Old Fougeras is a little demented. The bizarre letters he wrote to you in Saigon were the first indication.

'Gérapin's suicide did the rest.

'It's a case of repression, Troubert explains now, thereby enriching our vocabulary. He loved his young mistress of the manor too much, the old guard dog. Maybe he feared imaginary perils for her.

'He had done everything to bring her back to Nanteuil, and then to keep her there. He did not, as he told the commission, watch her leave the park five minutes after seeing me. He could not allow her to go.

'They abducted her and hid her in a secret room in the lodge. She attended the funeral the next day, veiled, whilst the police were searching for her.

'In fact, there were no unfortunate consequences. Your wife says she was treated with great consideration during her captivity. She refuses to file a complaint. So do you, I imagine?

'And so, case closed.'

'And if I'd refused?'

'Refused to see Mme. d'Arlon again because of that absurd incident? Bah! Triel and I would have taken care of her.'

'My wife is very lucky to have friends like you,' murmurs d'Arlon.

'It's the least we could do... Childhood friends, you know.'

D'Arlon smiles. It's the first time I've ever seen him smile freely, I think.

There's the sound of a horn in the street below.

'Are they here?'

But they aren't here yet.

*****

I often think back to that sunny moment, which lasted until two o'clock in the afternoon. I hear the squeal of brakes, the slam of a car door. I see once more Mme. d'Arlon in the doorway of the room, almost as pale as the first evening in Nanteuil. And d'Arlon, not really knowing what to say, or how to keep his composure....

My imagination sometimes has me wandering beneath the trees of Nanteuil. Triel and I have our means of access to that estate which will never more see any master. We hardly use them.

The Fougeras continue to maintain the park in mechanical fashion. When I encounter one or the other on a path, they keep their eyes averted.

The energies of the two old people are on the wane. The nettles, more vigorous than ever, gain ground every year. Already the manor is encircled. The sombre velvet army, in white bloom every spring, has almost reached the main gate.

From the d'Arlons, no news. A few deliberately banal letters from the young woman, less and less frequent.

What to believe? That the shadow of the old park continues to haunt them there, at the other end of the world?

One evening, near the stone bench, Triel threatened and brought to tears a young woman clad like a pauper. We dragged her out of her gloomy reverie and from her rest. We took her out of the lodge and threw her into the arms of someone who undoubtedly loved her, but in a clumsy and savage way.

But did she ever love René d'Arlon? Has she ever loved anyone, that child born into a life of lies? What were her feelings for the other one, the one she killed with her own hands? What was there in their common past? And are the simplest explanations the truest?

All such questions are in vain. We couldn't have acted any other way than the way we did. Triel says everything has worked out just fine the way it is.

Maybe he's right, once again.

But no footprint analysis can ever prove it.

The silence, I'd like to believe, is just the natural ingratitude of happy people.

But it might equally well be the silent reproach of two proud souls, bruised and forever turned in on themselves....

THE END